In the Kitchen with Pete & Rosa

Written for Fit Kids®
by
Kate Duffy & Sarah McRedmond

Illustrations created for Fit Kids®
by Pat Bagley

Design Consultation: Brian Jones

Fit Kids in the Kitchen with Pete & Rosa
copyright (c) 2002 by Kate Duffy & Sarah McRedmond
Fit Kids Publishing
175 West 200 South, Salt Lake City, Utah 84101
801-521-8321 801-521-8360 (fax)
www.fitkids.org

Special thanks to:

The George S. & Dore' Dolores
Eccles Foundation
Fred Meyer Foundation
Smith's Food & Drug
Bank One
Olney Alleneo
Meg Averett
The Ramsey Group
Ken & Julia Ament
BD Medical Systems
Bill Bennion
Brent Baker
Paul Boyd
Herschel & Lora Bullen
Steve Beierlein
Dale Bradley
Jill Bridges
Todd Butler
Greg Boyce
Steve Boyer
Brent Cameron
Rick Casey
Pete Cayias
Troy D'Ambrosia
Burt & Dorothy Dart
Paul Dougan
Bryan & Dave Eldridge

Jay Gamble
Doug Gaskill
Dean Gray
Bill Finney
Jerry Furhman
Daniel Flores
Ed Havas
Bill & Kathy Hyde
Kris Hofenbeck
Megan Hollbrook
Gil Iker
Magda Jacovcev-Ulrich
Ed Jamison
Community Bank of Nevada
Mary Jane Johnson
Dave Jones
Gary Juhlin
Dough Kruithof
Paul Liapis
Michael Marriott
Kent Larson
Tim Larson
Kent Lewis
Bruce & Patty Miller
Dan Miller
David Mong
Jerry Moore

Ted Nagata
Rich & RaNae Nordlund
Rick Ostler
Raplh Pahnke
Larry Pinnock
Dorothy Plesche
Tamara Pluth
Barbara Polich
Scott Rice
Arnie Richer
The Rosenblatt Fnd.
James Roberts
Herschel Saperstein
Edna Schettler
Brad Smith
Jim Steele
Marry Ellen Sloan
Bob Stayner
Sherrie Swensen
Stan Van Der Toolen
Ralph Wakley
Blaze Wharton
Fred Wheeler
Von White
John Williams
David Yocom
Dick Zito

ISBN 0-9709301-6-X
0 9 8 7 6 5 4 3 2 1
Printed and bound in the
United States of America

TABLE OF CONTENTS

GETTING STARTED

Kids need to eat healthy food to help their bodies work the way they should. If kids don't eat good food, pretty soon their bodies don't work properly and they can get tired and very sick.

Did you know that food can affect your mood? Too much sugar can make you hyper, or it can cause you to be mad or upset for no obvious reason? Too many preservatives in food can make you sick and cause you to be in a bad mood.

It's important to read the labels on all packaged food so you know what you're putting in your body.

Fit Kids in the Kitchen with Pete and Rosa was developed to help kids make decisions about what food is good for them and what food is not so good. This information will help them be better, healthier kids and grow up to be healthy adults. The recipes are easy to make and each one contains ingredients that will help kids get the right amount of nutrients every day.

GETTING STARTED

In this cookbook we've used sweeteners other than sugar wherever possible. They include fruit juice concentrate, honey and fresh or cooked fruit. When using fruit juice concentrate as a substitute for sugar, use naturally sweetened juice that does not contain sugar. Don't mix it with water. Use it just as is, right out of the can.

If a traditional recipe calls for 1 cup sugar you can use 1/3 cup fruit juice concentrate as a substitute. When using canned fruit, we recommend the type sweetened with fruit juice or in its own juice. The label will tell you the ingredients so you know whether or not it's the kind without sugar. We have not used any sugar substitutes such as saccharin or aspartame in these recipes.

Pete and Rosa use the food pyramid as a guideline for preparing healthy meals. You can learn all about the food pyramid and all about vitamins and minerals in The Food Pyramid and People Fuel chapters in this book.

Safety in the kitchen is very important. Kids and grownups need to wash their hands thoroughly before cooking or eating food.

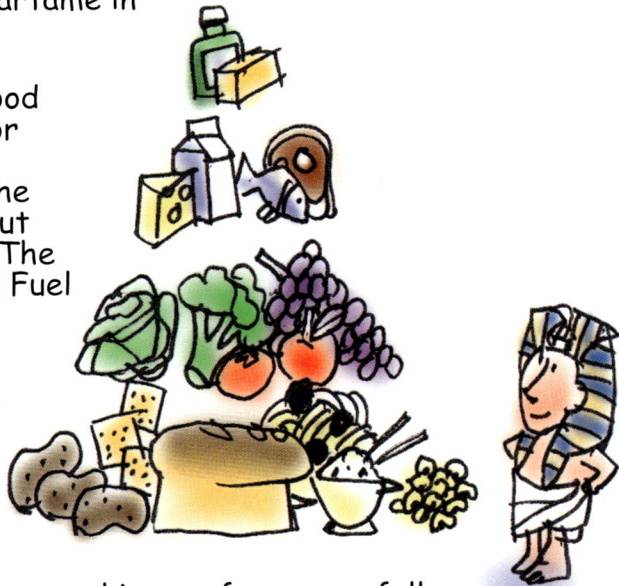

It's also important to clean cooking surfaces carefully, be aware of burn hazards in the kitchen, and be careful using kitchen utensils and equipment. We've included a chapter on kitchen safety in this book called Clean and Safe.

5

GETTING STARTED

Kids can learn many things from cooking. In addition to gaining math skills from measuring and mixing the recipes, they can learn a few things about science, like what happens when rice and water are combined with heat, or how leavening such as baking powder and baking soda can make muffins rise in the oven.

Using a cookbook can sharpen kids reading skills, too and make reading fun. Children can also learn about working as a group through cooking experiences. Cooking helps kids gain self-esteem, expands their tastes, gives them a glimpse of the differences in cultures, develops their imagination and, most importantly, kids can learn to make healthy food choices that will serve them well throughout their lives.

Most of the recipes in this book can be prepared by a child with a minimum amount of adult supervision. Children age 12 or younger should definitely have supervision when putting food in or taking it out of the oven, handling knives larger than a paring knife, using an electric mixer or blender, melting butter on the stove or in the microwave, and draining boiling water from pasta or potatoes.

READ THE CLEAN AND SAFE CHAPTER IN THIS BOOK FOR HELPFUL TIPS ON SAFETY IN THE KITCHEN.

We recommend adult supervision as a general rule, but not just as a safety precaution. Cooking is a good way for children and adults to spend quality time together.

Fit Kids and Pete and Rosa hope you have fun with this cookbook while you gain some valuable information about healthy food and good eating habits.

CLEAN AND SAFE

There are lots of things to know about being safe in the kitchen

Handwashing is a very important thing. Lots of bad germs can get in food when we prepare it with dirty hands. When we eat food prepared with dirty hands we can get very sick.

Food, especially meat and eggs, contain bacteria. When we handle these foods raw, the bacteria can be passed to other things we touch if we don't get it off our hands. This also applies to work surfaces and utensils used in preparing food.

Kids and grownups need to wash their hands

Before cooking or preparing any food

After touching or playing with pets

After using cleaning products

Before eating, drinking or snacking

After changing a diaper or the litter box

After contact with blood or other body fluids

After using the bathroom

After caring for someone who is sick

After coughing or sneezing

After handling garbage

After activities or playing

7

How to Wash Hands the Right Way

Use warm water

Use enough soap to make lots of lather

Get soap under fingernails and between fingers

Rub fingernails across palms

Rub hands together to create friction

Scrub 30 SECONDS in one direction and 30 SECONDS in the opposite direction

Rinse completely

Dry hands with a paper towel

Turn off faucet without touching it with your hand by using the paper towel

Throw towel away without touching the trash can

If you accidentally touch the faucet, inside of the sink or trash can with your clean hands, START OVER.

CLEAN AND SAFE

Kids should tie long hair back before preparing food. Shirt sleeves should be short. If they're long, roll them up securely so they won't get loose and get in the way. Long ties, scarves bandanas, ribbons or anything that hangs loose should be removed before cooking. It's a fire hazard.

Even if you are old enough to use the stovetop, oven or microwave, be sure to ask an adult to check you out on the equipment before you begin cooking. Young children need to have an adult or older sibling in the kitchen to help when using these appliances.

Always turn pan handles to the side when using the stove top. You don't want to accidentally bump them, tipping them over and spilling hot liquid. If you can, use the back burners.

Stir food in pots on the stove with a long-handled spoon. Don't stir too fast or it will splash.

Stand to the side of cooking pots instead of directly in front of them.

Kids should not stand on chairs or step-stools to use work surfaces or appliances in the kitchen.

CLEAN AND SAFE

Whenever possible, lower the work surface to the height a child can manage. If you have an electric skillet, use it instead of the stove wherever possible. It's safer.

Use caution when you remove the plastic wrap from a bowl or plate after it has been in the microwave. The steam comes out really fast. Get help draining boiling water from pasta or potatoes.

Steam can burn kids. Be careful when you remove the lid from a pot filled with hot liquid. Do it slowly and keep your hands and face away from the escaping steam.

Sharp knives, picks, graters, peelers and other kitchen tools can also be dangerous if not used properly. Young children need to have an adult or older sibling use this equipment for them.

Don't put anything into food unless you know what it is. It might be poisonous and could make you sick.

Oven coils get very hot. Don't touch them.

Keep paper towels, dish towels and other flammable materials away from burners and oven coils. They could catch on fire.

Gas stoves have an open flame. Always be careful when using a gas stove.

Grease can cause a fire if it spills onto the burner or meets the burner flame on a gas stove. Be careful with grease.

Kitchen fires should be put out with a fire extinguisher or baking soda. Don't pour water on a kitchen fire. It will cause it to spread.

Get help putting things in and taking things out of the oven.

NO PUSHING OR SHOVING IN THE KITCHEN! THIS IS NOT A GOOD PLACE TO PLAY AND NO FIGHTING IS ALLOWED!

PEOPLE FUEL

Our bodies need fuel to work at their best. People get fuel from food. Each of the body's organs has a specific purpose and all of the body's organs work together to keep us healthy.

Our body parts get nourishment from nutrients like vitamins, minerals, protein and carbohydrates that come from food. The food pyramid recommends that we eat a specific number of servings from different food groups each day. Here's why.

Each serving of the food from each food group supplies a percentage or a portion of the nutrients necessary for the body to work properly for the entire day. Eating good food sometimes and food that's not so good for us the rest of the time doesn't help the body.

We need good food in the recommended amount everyday to get the nutrients necessary to remain healthy.

Here is a list of some of the vitamins, minerals, carbohydrates and protein we need everyday, along with an explanation of what some of these nutrients do, and some foods that they come from.

The food we eat is very important because these nutrients aren't available to the body from anywhere else. In addition to eating good food, we need to drink plenty of fresh, clean water to stay healthy.

Some Important Minerals

Calcium helps bones, teeth, the heart, blood, muscles and kidneys. We get calcium from milk, yogurt, tofu, kale and collard greens.

Magnesium helps the heart and blood, and promotes vitamin and mineral absorption. We get magnesium from bran, avocados, almonds, shredded wheat, pumpkin seeds, peanuts, peanut butter, bananas, raisins, shrimp, baked potatoes, cashews, oat and bran cereals, spinach, kiwi, hummus, broccoli, whole wheat bread, lentils and wheat germ.

Iron is good for our blood, lungs and muscles. We get iron from spinach, beet greens, broccoli, kale, prunes, whole wheat bread, meat and poultry.

Folic Acid is necessary for the body's cells, blood and metabolism. Folic acid is found in dried beans and peas, lentils, fresh oranges and orange juice, whole wheat bread, liver, asparagus, beets, broccoli, Brussels sprouts and spinach.

Copper helps our bodies absorb minerals. It also builds muscles, blood cells, and bones. Copper is found in liver, shrimp, oysters, crab, almonds, black and kidney beans and brown rice.

Zinc heals wounds and helps our muscles, blood and tissues. It also aids digestion. We get zinc from black beans, black-eyed peas, lentils, soybeans, eggs, milk, chicken, liver, wheat germ and collard greens.

Manganese gives us energy, helps the blood, aids vitamin absorption and breaks down fats and cholesterol. It's also important for the nerves and our brain. Foods like almonds, dried apricots, bananas, brown rice, cashews, collard greens, kale, soybeans and whole wheat bread provide manganese.

Potassium is necessary for the health of our brain, kidneys, blood and heart. Prunes, raisins, raw spinach, bananas, pork, artichokes, tomatoes and chicken supply our bodies with potassium.

Selenium is important for the body's cells and tissues. We get selenium from brown rice, chicken, ground beef, liver, tuna and salmon, eggs, tofu, soybeans and whole wheat bread.

Some Important Vitamins

Vitamin A/Beta Carotene repairs tissue, skin, lungs, the throat, eyes, mouth and nose, bones and teeth. The foods with Vitamin A are apricots, cantaloupe, broccoli, carrots, collard greens, kale, red peppers, spinach, sweet potatoes, tomatoes, winter squash, milk, eggs, liver and oatmeal.

Vitamin B1/Thiamin aids metabolism, energy and digestion, and helps the nerves, muscles and the heart. We get Vitamin B1 from beef, salmon, liver, pumpernickel bread, wheat germ, black beans and whole wheat bread.

Vitamin B2/Riboflavin is good for the blood and other cells. It builds antibodies and helps our eyesight. Milk, yogurt, spinach, kale, green beans, collard greens, liver, beef, salmon, eggs, cashews, almonds and black beans are a good source of Vitamin B2.

Vitamin B3/Niacin aids circulation, reduces cholesterol, gives us energy and helps our skin and blood pressure. Foods with Vitamin B3 are almonds, dried apricots, chicken, liver, tuna, salmon, milk, yogurt and oatmeal.

Vitamin B6/Pyridoxine is important for our metabolism. It also builds antibodies, aids the central nervous system, keeps our skin healthy and helps balance minerals. Some foods containing Vitamin B6 are bananas, black beans, green beans, cashews, kidney beans, chicken, salmon, ground beef, liver and pumpernickel bread.

Vitamin B12 is important for our blood cells, metabolism and nerves. It is important for growth in children. Vitamin B12 also helps with calcium absorption and gives us energy. We get this vitamin from cottage cheese, chicken, ground beef, liver, eggs, milk and yogurt.

Vitamin C/Ascorbic Acid is important for healthy teeth, gums and bones. It also helps heal wounds and helps fight infection. Vitamin C is also necessary for blood vessels and the absorption of iron and collagen. The foods with Vitamin C include apricots, broccoli, winter squash, strawberries, oranges and orange juice, cauliflower, kale and red peppers.

Vitamin E builds cells, blood and is good for the heart. Eat asparagus, almonds, collard greens, kale, spinach and wheat germ to get Vitamin E.

Fat stores energy, builds nerves and protects organs. Fats from vegetables, rather than animals, are best. For example, when cooking with oil it is best to use olive oil, corn or other vegetable oil instead of butter or lard.

Carbohydrates give our bodies energy. We get carbohydrates from fruit, vegetables, rice, cereal, pasta, bread and potatoes.

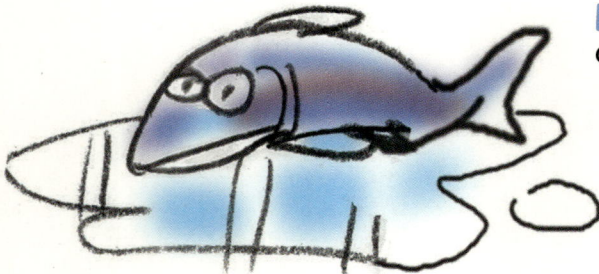

Protein is very important for our bodies. It repairs the body and helps us grow. We get protein from nuts, brown rice, whole wheat bread, eggs, milk, cheese, yogurt, fish, meat, beans and soybeans.

The Food Pyramid

The Pyramid divides food into five major food groups: grains, vegetables, fruits, milk and dairy, and meat.

Sweets and fats are at the very top.   We need these in very small quantities.

Each of these food groups provides some, but not all, of the nutrients and energy kids need to keep their bodies healthy.

All the major food groups are important and none of the major food groups is more important than another.

For good health and proper growth, you'll need to eat a variety of different foods every day.

As you look at the food groups, remember that a simple sandwich might contain one or more servings from several food groups.

GRAIN

Grain products provide vitamins, minerals, complex carbohydrates and dietary fiber. Kids need six servings from this group each day. Three of these servings should come from enriched grain foods and three from whole grain foods. Here are some examples of foods from this food group and the amounts needed to make a serving:

WHOLE GRAIN
1 /2 cup cooked brown rice
2-3 graham crackers
5-6 whole grain crackers
1/2 cup cooked oatmeal
1/2 cup cooked bulgur
3 cups popped popcorn
3 rice or popcorn cakes
1 ounce ready-to-eat whole grain cereal
1 slice pumpernickel, rye or whole wheat bread
2 taco shells
1 7-inch flour tortilla

ENRICHED GRAIN
1/2 cup cooked rice or pasta
1/2 cup cooked spaghetti
1/2 English muffin or bagel
1 slice white, wheat, French or Italian bread
1/2 hamburger or hotdog bun
1 small dinner roll
6 crackers (soda cracker size)
1 4-inch pita bread
1 4-inch pancake
1 /2 cup cooked grits
1 /2 cup cooked farina or other cereal
9 small pretzels
1 ounce ready-to-eat, non sugar-coated cereal

VEGETABLES

The vegetable group is very important! Kids need 3 to 5 servings a day for vitamins, minerals and dietary fiber. The amounts shown equal one serving.

VEGETABLE GROUP CHOICES

DARK-GREEN LEAFY
1 /2 cup cooked collard greens
1 cup leafy raw vegetables
romaine lettuce, spinach, or
mixed green salad
2 cooked broccoli spears
1 /2 cup cooked turnip greens,
kale or mustard greens

DEEP-YELLOW
1 1/2 whole carrots, cooked
7-8 raw carrot sticks (3" long)
1 /2 cup winter squash

STARCHY
1 medium ear of corn
1 medium baked potato
1 /2 cup green peas
1 /2 cup lima beans
1 medium plantain

DRY BEANS & PEAS
1 /2 cup cooked black, kidney,
pinto or garbanzo beans, or
black-eyed peas
1 /2 cup cooked lentils
1 cup bean soup
1 /2 cup cooked split peas

OTHER GOOD VEGETABLES
1 /3 medium cucumber
9 raw snow or sugar pea pods
1 /2 cup cooked green beans
4 medium Brussels sprouts
1 /2 cup coleslaw
1 /2 cup cooked cabbage
7-8 celery sticks (3" long)
1 /2 cup tomato or spaghetti
sauce
3 /4 cup vegetable juice
1 cup vegetable soup
1 medium tomato
5 cherry tomatoes

FRUITS

The fruit group is very important too! Kids should eat plenty of these foods for vitamins, minerals and dietary fiber. It is recommended that you eat 2 to 4 servings daily from this food group. The amount that makes a serving is listed with the fruit.

FRUIT GROUP CHOICES

CITRUS, MELONS AND BERRIES

1 /2 cup blueberries or raspberries
1 /4 medium cantaloupe
3 /4 cup orange juice
1/2 grapefruit
1 /8 medium honeydew
1 large kiwi fruit
1 medium orange
7 medium strawberries
1 medium tangerine
1 /2 cup watermelon pieces

OTHER GOOD FRUITS INCLUDE

1 medium apple, banana, peach, or nectarine
2 medium apricots
11 cherries
1 /4 cup dried fruit
1 /2 cup applesauce
2 1/2 slices canned pineapple
12 grapes
1 /2 medium mango
1 /4 medium papaya
1 small pear

18

MILK AND DAIRY

Foods from the milk and dairy group are important for calcium. One serving from this group is based on the amount of calcium in 1 cup of milk.

You'll need 2 to 3 servings from this group each day. The following foods in the amounts indicated equal one serving. If you don't want that much of the individual food for a serving, use your math skills to figure out what portion of the serving you'll get from a smaller portions. EXAMPLE: You would have to eat 2 cups of cottage cheese to equal one serving from the milk and dairy group. If you eat 1/2 cup of cottage cheese, that's 1/4 of a milk and dairy group serving.

1 cup milk
1 cup soy milk, calcium fortified
1 cup yogurt (8 ounces)
1 1/2 ounces natural cheese
2 ounces processed cheese
1 1/3 ounces string cheese
2 cups cottage cheese
1 1/2 cups ice cream
1 cup frozen yogurt
1 cup pudding

MEAT

The meat group includes protein sources such as eggs, dry beans, peas, peanut butter, poultry and fish.

These foods are important for protein, iron, and zinc. Two to three ounces of cooked lean meat, poultry or fish equal one serving from this group. Count 1 egg or 1/2 cup cooked dry beans as 1 ounce of lean meat or 1/3 to 1/2 of a serving. Count 2 tablespoons peanut butter as 1 ounce of meat. You need 2 to 3 servings from this food group every day.

THESE FOODS ARE LISTED BY OUNCES. REMEMBER THAT YOU'LL NEED 2 TO 3 OUNCES TO MAKE A SERVING.

2 ounces cooked lean meat = 2 ounces
2 ounces cooked poultry or fish = 2 ounces
1 egg (yolk and white) = 1 ounce
2 tablespoons peanut butter = 1 ounce
1 1/2 frankfurters = 1 ounce
2 slices bologna or luncheon meat = 1 ounce
1/4 cup drained canned salmon or tuna = 1 ounce
1/2 cup cooked kidney, pinto or white beans = 1 ounce
1/2 cup tofu = 1 ounce
1 soy burger patty = 1 ounce

FATS AND SWEETS

The small tip of the pyramid shows that it is best to eat only a small amount of food that contains fat and sugars. These foods contain calories but few vitamins and minerals.
To satisfy your sweet tooth, check out the recipes in the Healthy Sweet Treats chapter.

PETE AND ROSA'S EXCELLENT ADVENTURE

Going to the grocery store to shop for food can be great fun, but how do you know what to buy? Here are some steps to follow that will help you get the right ingredients for your recipes.

Pete and Rosa know how to make shopping an excellent adventure so let's get started. The first thing we need to do is plan a menu. Kids can do this easily. Get paper and pencil and start with breakfast. What sounds good for breakfast? Is it healthy? How many food groups does it include? Check it out using the food pyramid. You can read about it in the Food Pyramid chapter.

Now, move on to lunch and then to snacks and dinner. Don't forget dessert. You're in charge so put your favorite foods on the menu. Be sure to include the healthy foods that you especially like to eat. To find out what vitamins and minerals are in what foods, read the People Fuel Chapter.

Here's a sample:

Breakfast
 Scrambled Eggs in a Jar (page 32) served with orange juice and a slice of whole wheat toast.

Lunch
Crunchy Fruity Pizza (page 44) served with carrot and celery sticks on the side and a glass of milk.

Snack
Ants on a Log (page 80)

Dinner
Gobbler Cobbler (page 54) served with a tossed green salad, roll and a glass of milk.

Sweet Treat for Dessert
Upside Down Fruit Crunch (page 93)

Got your menu? Now you're ready to make a grocery list. Look at each menu item and write down the ingredients you'll need. You'll already have some things on hand. Check the cupboards, refrigerator and freezer for ingredients before you put them on the list.

Breakfast

For Scrambled Eggs in a Jar served with orange juice and a slice of whole wheat toast, you'll need eggs, milk, butter, cheese and whole wheat bread for toast. Don't forget the orange juice!

Lunch

Crunchy Fruity Pizza served with carrot and celery sticks on the side and a glass of milk. Let's make it this time with vanilla yogurt and fresh peaches. You'll need 4 rice cakes, 1 carton of yogurt and 2 medium-sized fresh peaches. You'll also need some carrots and celery. Check the refrigerator to see if you have milk on hand.

Snack

Ants on a Log
Requires peanut butter, raisins and celery.

Dinner

Gobbler Cobbler calls for a frozen pie crust, leftover turkey (you can also make this with leftover chicken), frozen peas, a small onion, a small apple, 2 cans cream of chicken soup, raisins, nutmeg, lemon juice and butter. Check the cupboard to see what you have on hand. Add the ingredients you don't have to your list. How about rolls? Do you need to add them?

Sweet Treat for Dessert

Upside Down Fruit Crunch
This time let's use pineapple. You'll need a can of pineapple chunks in natural juice. Check the cupboard to see if you have flour. If not, add it to the list. You'll also need eggs, pecans, a little butter and frozen fruit juice sweetened with fruit.

"Lots of the vitamins, minerals and carbohydrates we need every day come from foods found in the grocer's produce department. Our bodies need 3 to 5 servings of vegetables every day and 2 to 4 servings of fruit."

" Vitamins work with Enzymes in our body to turn fat and carbohydrates into energy, form bones, tissue, blood cells and our genes. Minerals from fruits and vegetables balance fluid in the body, regulate the heartbeat and help the blood carry oxygen to all parts of the body. Some vitamins in fruits and vegetables help fight off disease."

IF YOU USE CANNED FRUITS AND VEGETABLES, MAKE SURE YOU READ THE LABEL. YOU DON'T WANT TOO MUCH ADDED SUGAR, SALT OR TOO MANY INGREDIENTS YOU AREN'T FAMILIAR WITH.

SEE IF THERE'S A FARMERS MARKET WHERE YOU LIVE. A TRIP TO THE FARMER'S MARKET ON SATURDAY IS GREAT FUN AND A GOOD PLACE TO BUY FRESH PRODUCE.

"The store has lots of oils for cooking and to add to foods. We get fat from cooking oils but we also get fat from some of the food we eat.
Meat, cheese and milk all have fat. Fats store energy from the food we eat, carry vitamins around in the body, and build nerves and the membranes around cells."

"Fatty tissues help protect many organs in our body. We need fat in our diet every day, but we need good fat and in small amounts.
It's best to get most of the fat we eat from vegetable sources and just a little bit from animal sources."

"This part of the store has bread, cereal, rice and grains. We get carbohydrates from this food group. Carbohydrates give our bodies energy."

"There are goodies here too. Cookies, cakes and candies. It's okay to eat a little bit of sugar but these foods are very high in sugar. You can't make a meal out of cookies or candy or ice cream. They have a lot of empty calories."

"Wow! I love to come to the grocery store. Look at all this good healthy food we bought. And we have everything we need to make our delicious recipes. Let's get started."

IN PLACE OF SUGAR, SWEETEN TREATS WITH HONEY, JAM SWEETENED WITH FRUIT JUICE, FRESH AND COOKED FRUIT AND FRUIT JUICE CONCENTRATE. READ THE LABELS ON CANNED FRUIT TO SEE HOW ITS SWEETENED.

BREAKFAST

Breakfast is the most important meal of the day. When you start the day with a good breakfast, your body is fueled with energy and the important nutrients that will get you going. You'll learn better in school, have more fun at play and get along better with others if you eat a healthy breakfast. Pete and Rosa always eat a good breakfast, even when they're in a hurry. The recipes in this chapter are simple and have the right kinds of ingredients to get you off to a good start.

BEFORE WE BEGIN, REMEMBER TO WASH YOUR HANDS! IF THE RECIPE YOU'RE MAKING REQUIRES HELP FROM AN ADULT, BE SURE YOU HAVE DISCUSSED THEIR PARTICIPATION BEFORE YOU START. FOR SAFETY TIPS IN THE KITCHEN, READ THE CLEAN AND SAFE CHAPTER.

ROSA'S WARM YOUR TUMMY OATMEAL

Oatmeal is a simple breakfast but it's a great way to warm up on a chilly morning. This recipe uses plain instant oatmeal with no flavoring or sugar added. Sounds kind of boring, but Rosa makes it exciting by adding her own delicious and healthy ingredients for a nutritious and good-tasting Fit Kids breakfast.

You'll need:
- a microwave-safe bowl
- measuring spoons
- a butter knife

Ingredients:

1 package plain instant oatmeal, or instant oatmeal from a box one or more of the following:
1/3 cup raisins
1/2 teaspoon cinnamon
1/3 cup chopped nuts (walnuts are good or use almonds, cashews or peanuts)
1 small sliced banana
1 small fresh apple, peach, pear or mango cut into bite size pieces

Yield: 1 serving
Time: under 5 minutes

Instructions:

Cook oatmeal according to the package directions. When the oatmeal is done, mix in one or more of the ingredients. Top it off with a drizzle of honey or a dab of jam sweetened with fruit juice instead of sugar. Add milk if you like. Yummy in the tummy!

Waffles Your Way

Pete sure likes to have things his own way. That's why these waffles are one of his favorite breakfasts. Here's a recipe to make your own special waffles. This recipe uses packaged waffle mix. If you don't eat all of the waffles, put them in a plastic sandwich bag when they are cool and freeze them for another time. Just pop frozen waffles into the toaster for homemade waffles in a hurry. If you don't have a waffle iron, make "Pancakes Your Way" using this same method.

You'll need:
- a waffle iron (griddle for pancakes)
- a mixing bowl
- measuring cups and spoons
- a butter knife
- a wooden spoon
- a spatula

Ingredients:

packaged waffle mix
oil or non-stick cooking spray
fresh fruit
butter
honey or fruit-sweetened jam
yogurt or applesauce

Instructions:

Prepare waffle mix (or pancake mix if you don't have a waffle iron) according to package directions.
Add 3/4 cup of one of the following ingredients to the mix: fresh fruit including bananas, drained pineapple chunks, berries, chopped apples, chopped nuts. A pinch of cinnamon in the batter is good with apples and nuts. Canned fruit can be used in this recipe. Be sure it's the kind sweetened with fruit juice instead of sugar. Drain the fruit well before adding to the batter. If you're feeling creative, use a combination of ingredients but be sure they will go together before you add them. Mix the additions gently into the waffle mix, especially the berries, so they don't get too squished. Cook waffles (or pancakes) according the directions on the package. Be sure to have an adult help you if you're not old enough to use small appliances on your own. When the waffles are done, top them with melted butter, plain or flavored yogurt, more fruit, or applesauce. It's best to use applesauce that doesn't contain sugar. It tastes better than the sweetened kind.

29

Greens, Eggs and Ham

This recipe covers quite a few food groups and it's fun and easy to make.

You'll need:
- a small skillet with a lid or an egg poacher
- a slotted spatula
- a Tablespoon

Ingredients:

1 egg
1 slice deli ham
1 cheese single
1/2 English muffin
1/2 cup leftover green vegetable such as spinach, broccoli or peas
dab of butter or cooking spray

Instructions:

Remove ham, cheese and vegtables from refrigerator and place on counter to warm up. Grease the bottom of the skillet with a dab of butter or cooking spray. Place the pan on the burner and turn to high. Crack egg in the pan and when it starts to cook add one Tablespoon of water. Cover with the lid and turn the burner off. Place the English muffin on a plate. Layer leftover vegetables, then ham and then cheese on the muffin. Check on the egg. When the white part is cooked, remove from the pan with the spatula and place on top of muffin. If the veggies are really cold, heat in the microwave for one minute before placing on the muffin.

Surprise Muffins

Surprise muffins are a great treat for breakfast or as a snack. The surprise is a yummy piece of fruit in the center. Almost any kind of fruit will work for these muffins: fresh, canned or dried is fine so long as it is cut into small pieces.

You'll need:

- 2 mixing bowls (one should be medium-size, the other microwave safe)
- a wooden spoon
- measuring cups and spoons
- a butter knife
- a muffin pan
- oven mitts
- cooking spray, oil or cupcake papers

Ingredients:

1 1/2 cups flour
2 teaspoons baking powder
1/2 teaspoon baking soda
1/2 teaspoon salt
2 eggs
1 cup milk
1/2 teaspoon vanilla
4 Tablespoons melted butter
1/4 cup honey or fruit sweetened jam
3 Tablespoons honey to roll fruit in
12 (quarter size) pieces of fruit like berries, apricots or apple

Yield: 1 dozen muffins
Time: 25 - 30 minutes

Instructions:

Set the oven to 375 degrees. In a medium-size mixing bowl add the flour, baking powder, baking soda, salt and sugar. Set this aside. With a butter knife, cut 4 Tablespoons butter and place in a small microwave-safe bowl. Heat for 30 - 45 seconds until melted. Careful. It's hot! Add 1 cup milk to the butter. Crack two eggs into the milk and add 1/2 teaspoon vanilla. Mix well. Pour the wet ingredients into the dry ingredients you set aside earlier, then stir everything together with a wooden spoon. Mix it up good.
Rub the muffin cups with shortening or use cooking spray or cupcake papers. Fill muffin cups half full. Roll the fruit in honey then push the fruit pieces into the center of each muffin. Put the pan into the oven and bake for 15 minutes. When the muffins are golden brown, use the oven mitts to take them out.   Cool for 10 – 15 minutes before eating.

Scrambled Eggs in a Jar

This is a healthy way to start the morning and lots of fun too! Serve these Fit Kids scrambled eggs with toast and fresh fruit or juice.

You'll need:
- a clean 1 quart wide mouth jar with lid
- a skillet
- a wooden spoon
- a spatula
- a butter knife
- measuring cups
- a cheese grater

Ingredients:

4 eggs
1/4 cup low fat milk
pinch of pepper
1 Tablespoon butter
1/4 cup shredded cheddar cheese
optional: 1/4 cup of pre-cooked ham, diced

Yield: 2 servings
Time: 10 minutes

Instructions:

Crack the eggs into the jar. Add milk, cheese and a pinch of black pepper. Put the lid on the jar. Be sure it's on tight. Meanwhile, place a skillet on the stove over medium heat. Spray the pan with cooking spray or use 1 Tablespoon butter. Move it around the skillet with a butter knife so it coats the whole bottom surface.
Now comes the fun part. Shake the jar up and down to mix up all the ingredients. Not too hard!
When the ingredients are mixed well, remove the lid and pour the mixture into the pan. Gently stir the eggs with a wooden spoon until they are cooked. Transfer to a plate and you are ready to fuel up for morning.

Baby Burritos
Use the recipe for eggs in a jar to make this tasty breakfast treat

You'll also need:

2 flour tortillas
1/2 cup mild salsa

Make scrambled eggs in a jar from the recipe on page 32. While the eggs are cooking, place the tortillas on plates. Divide the cooked eggs, half on one tortilla and half on the other.

Add 1/4 salsa to each, spreading it to the edges of the egg and tortilla. Now roll it up. Place the edge side down on the plate and cut into bite-size pieces with a butter knife.

Bread Pudding Muffins

These muffins are good on cold mornings. They're easy to make and have an old fashioned taste. The perfect way to start a Fit Kids day.

You'll need:
- 2 mixing bowls, one that is microwave-safe
- a wooden spoon
- measuring cups and spoons
- a muffin pan
- cooking spray, oil or cupcake papers
- oven mitts

Ingredients:

12 slices whole wheat bread cut into 1-inch cubes
1 cup lowfat milk
4 large eggs
2/3 cup raisins
1 Tablespoon vanilla fruit juice concentrate
2 Tablespoons melted butter
1 Tablespoon ground cinnamon

Yield: 12 muffins
Time: 15 minutes

Instructions:

Put the bread cubes into a large mixing bowl. Measure the raisins and add them to the bread. Set this aside. Melt the butter in the microwave-safe bowl for 30 - 45 seconds. Add milk, eggs, cinnamon and vanilla to the butter and mix well.
Pour the milk mixture over the bread and mix together with the wooden spoon.
Let the bread sit in the milk mixture for 5 minutes until it has soaked in well. Preheat oven to 350 degrees.
Spray the muffin pan with cooking spray or grease the cups with shortening. Don't grease the cups if you use cupcake papers. Fill the cups with the bread-milk mixture. Put them in the oven for 35 minutes. The muffins are done when they are firm and browned. Cool the muffins for at least 10 minutes before serving. These are good topped with jam. Jam sweetened with fruit will make this even more wholesome.

French Toast

When Pete makes French toast he says all the ingredients using his made-up French accent. He's not very good at it but Rosa thinks he's funny. French toast is an American dish. The French make something similar, called pain perdu, but the name translates to 'lost bread' in English.

This recipe calls for 1-inch thick slices of white bread but any kind of bread that sounds good to you will work. Pete doesn't recommend garlic bread. Cinnamon raisin bread and whole wheat are Rosa's favorites.

You'll need:
- a skillet
- a mixing bowl
- measuring cups and spoons
- a spatula

Ingredients:

2 eggs
1/2 cup milk
4 slices 1/2-inch thick bread
1 or 2 Tablespoons butter (for the pan)
or use cooking spray

Yield: 4 servings
Time: 30 minutes

Instructions:

Break the eggs into a pie pan or shallow dish. Measure the milk and add it to the eggs. Mix this up well. Place the skillet on the stove over medium-low heat. Put a pat or two of butter in the pan and let it melt (move it around with a knife so the pan gets coated with the butter). Or coat the pan with cooking spray. Dip a slice of bread into the egg mixture. Soak on one side then turn it over and soak the other side. This weakens the bread so be careful when you take it out of the bowl or it will fall apart.

When the pan is hot, place the soaked slice of bread into the pan. Reduce the heat to low and cook until it is brown underneath. Turn it over with a spatula and cook the same way on the other side.

Have a plate ready.
When the French toast is done, carefully take it out of the pan and place it on the plate. Serve it hot with syrup, jam sweetened with fruit or top with yogurt and sliced fruit.

Pete's Breakfast Rockets

This is a fast and easy way to get a healthy start on the day. Breakfast rockets can even be made the night before and put in the refrigerator. A great breakfast for Fit Kids on the go.

You'll need:
- plastic wrap
- Popsicle sticks
- measuring spoons and cups
- a wooden spoon or hand mixer

Ingredients:

1/2 cup plain or vanilla lowfat yogurt
1 Tablespoon peanut butter
2 teaspoons honey
1 cup granola
4 small bananas

Yield: 4 servings
Time: 10 minutes

Instructions:

Place yogurt, peanut butter and honey into a small mixing bowl and blend them together. Lay 4 large squares of plastic wrap on the table or counter.
Put 1/4 cup granola on each square. Peel the bananas and put a Popsicle stick in one end of each of the bananas, just like a Popsicle.
Coat each of the bananas with the yogurt mixture and then roll them in the granola.
Wrap each rocket in the plastic wrap square and refrigerate until you are ready to eat them.

Breakfast Parfait

Pete and Rosa love to make this special breakfast when they're in a hurry. If you put it in a plastic container with a lid, you can have breakfast on the go.

You'll need:
- a small bowl
- measuring cups

Ingredients:

3/4 cup plain or vanilla yogurt
a handful of your favorite granola
1/2 cup of your favorite berries

Yield: 1 serving
Time: less than 5 minutes

Instructions:

Put a scoop of yogurt in the bottom of a small bowl using about 1/4 of the carton (you can also use a parfait or sundae dish). Top with 1/2 of the granola. Place another scoop of yogurt, about 1/4 of carton on top of granola. Top with 1/2 of the berries. Add another 1/4 carton yogurt and top with remaining granola. Add another scoop of yogurt on top of this, then add remaining berries.

Cinnamon Soldiers

This is a hurry-up breakfast that Rosa learned about from her Fit Kids friends in England.

You'll need:
- a butter knife,
- toaster
- a small bowl

Ingredients:

2 pieces white bread
2 Tablespoons butter
1 teaspoon cinnamon
1 teaspoon honey

Yield: 8 cinnamon soldiers
Time: 5 minutes

Instruction:

Toast the bread. When it's done, spread butter on one side of each piece of toast with a butter knife. Measure the cinnamon and honey into a small bowl and mix them together. Spread the mixture on the toast. Going from the top crust to the bottom, cut each piece into three strips. You can march these little soldiers right up to your mouth.

Breakfast Smoothie

Smoothies aren't just for snacks. They make a wholesome breakfast too. This recipe offers the basic guidelines. You can add whatever ingredients you like.

You'll need:
- measuring cups and spoons
- a blender
- a paring knife

Ingredients:

1/2 cup plain or vanilla yogurt
1/2 cup low fat milk
1 Tablespoon honey
1/4 cup blueberries
1 banana
1/2 cup strawberries

Yield: 1 smoothie
Time: 5 minutes

Instructions:
Measure the yogurt, milk and honey into the blender. Wash the fruit, peel the banana and cut the tops off the strawberries. Add to the blender. Put the lid on tight and blend together for one minute. When well blended pour into an 8-ounce glass and serve.

Easy Omelets

The firm texture of this omelet makes it much easier for kids to make. Pete and Rosa like this for a special weekend breakfast.

You'll need:
- a skillet
- a small mixing bowl
- measuring cups and spoons
- a spatula
- cheese grater
- a fork

Ingredients:

2 eggs, beaten
2 Tablespoons low fat milk
1/8 teaspoon salt
1/4 cup cheddar cheese, shredded
1/4 cup diced tomato
1 green onion, chopped
1 Tablespoon butter

Yield: 1 large omelet
Time: 10 minutes

Instructions:

Set the skillet on the stove and turn the temperature to medium low. Place the butter in the skillet, moving it around with a butter knife so that the whole bottom is greased. Wash the vegetables and chop them up. Crack the eggs into a small bowl and beat with a fork until they are well blended and fluffy.

Add the eggs to the skillet and let them cook a few minutes until the edges start to turn up. Place the vegetables down the center of the egg mixture. Put the cheese on top of the vegetables. When the cheese is melted and the eggs aren't runny anymore, fold the omelet in half. Serve with your favorite toast. Optional: In place of or in addition to the tomato, add 1/4 cup grated carrots and zucchini.

LUNCH

Lunch offers lots of tempting possibilities. This is an important meal because the nutritious food we eat mid-day helps keep our bodies going. The recipes we've provided here are fun to eat and most are very easy to make.

Bumble Bee Sandwiches

You can use whatever filling you like for bumble bee sandwiches. Pete's favorite combination is bologna and cheese. Rosa likes peanut butter and jam. She uses jam sweetened with fruit instead of sugar.
Use your imagination to make your own special bumble bee sandwiches. We've used bologna and cheese in this recipe.

You'll need:
- a butter knife
- a cutting board or other clean work surface

Ingredients:

2 slices whole wheat bread
2 slice white bread
2 slices bologna
2 slices cheddar cheese
3 Tablespoons mayonnaise

Yield: 2 bumble bee
          sandwiches
Time: 10 minutes

Instructions:
Place all four slices of bread on the counter or work surface and spread them with mayonnaise. Place a piece of bologna on each piece of wheat bread, then add a slice of cheese. Top the wheat bread with a slice of white bread. With a butter knife, cut each sandwich into three strips. Look! Stripy bumble bees.

BEFORE WE BEGIN, REMEMBER TO WASH YOUR HANDS!
IF THE RECIPE YOU'RE MAKING REQUIRES HELP FROM AN ADULT, BE SURE YOU HAVE DISCUSSED THEIR PARTICIPATION BEFORE YOU START. FOR SAFETY TIPS IN THE KITCHEN, READ THE CLEAN AND SAFE CHAPTER.

Pete's Extra Special Grilled Cheese Sandwich

This is a yummy twist on an old favorite and makes a super Fit Kids lunch.

You'll need:
- a skillet
- a butter knife
- a paring knife
- a mixing bowl
- measuring spoons
- a spatula

Ingredients:

1 large apple, chopped
3 Tablespoons mayonnaise
4 slices cheddar cheese
2 slices cooked ham
2 Tablespoons butter
4 slices bread

Yield: 2 sandwiches
Time: 10 minutes

Instructions:

Wash the apple and cut it into bite-size pieces. Put the apples into a small bowl and add the mayonnaise. Mix well, making certain you completely coat the apples. Set two slices of bread on the counter or working surface. Place one slice of cheese on each piece of bread. Top each with the apple mixture, dividing it equally. Add a ham slice to each. Place the remaining slices of bread on top of each sandwich. Butter the outside of the top slice of bread. Put a skillet on the stove and heat it on medium. Place the sandwiches in the pan, butter side down. Butter the top slice of bread while the bottom cooks. Watch your fingers because the pan is hot! When golden brown on the bottom, turn to brown the other side. Serve with carrot and celery sticks.

Rosa's Power Roll-ups

Roll-ups are easy to make and fun too! Best of all, they're really good for you because each ingredient represents something from each food group found on the food pyramid. Pack them in your school lunch, take them on a picnic or make them for an after school snack.

You'll need:
- a small grater
- a small bowl
- a butter knife
- measuring spoons

Ingredients:

1 large flour tortilla
1 Tablespoon peanut butter
2 Tablespoons raisins
2 Tablespoons grated carrots
2 Tablespoons vanilla yogurt

Yield: 1 roll-up
Time: 5 minutes

Instructions:
Wash the carrot and carefully grate into a small bowl. Graters have sharp edges so watch your fingers. Place the tortilla on a plate and spread peanut butter to cover. Sprinkle the carrot and raisins over the peanut butter. With a spoon, drizzle the yogurt over the top and then roll it up. Cut in half and gobble it up.

Deep Sea Wrap Ups

These happy wraps are easy to make and good to eat.
In this recipe we've suggested using tortillas. You can also
use Naan, which is a flat East Indian bread. It's perfect
for these Fit Kids sandwiches.

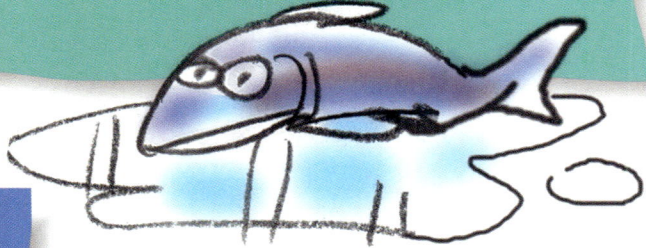

You'll need:
- a can opener
- a butter knife
- a paring knife
- a small bowl
- a fork
- measuring spoons

Ingredients:

1 can tuna
3 Tablespoons mayonnaise
1 chopped green onion or 1 stalk celery, chopped
1 chopped pickle or 2 teaspoons pickle relish (optional)
2 tortillas or 2 pieces Naan bread

Yield: 2 wraps
Time: 15 minutes

Instructions:
Open the can and drain the liquid from the tuna. Be careful, the lid is sharp around the edges. Spoon tuna into a small bowl and break it up with a fork. Get help chopping the onion, celery and pickle if you need it.
Add these to the tuna, then measure and add the mayonnaise.
Mix well. Set out 2 plates and put a tortilla or pieces of Naan bread on each. Scoop the tuna mixture onto the tortillas or Naan, spreading it to the edges. Roll and eat.

Crunchy Fruity Pizza

This recipe is made with rice cakes. The cream cheese makes them yummy and not as dry as eating them plain. Berries are excellent on Crunchy Fruity Pizza. Add banana slices for a real treat. Try making a rainbow with strawberries, orange slices, banana, kiwi fruit and blueberries!

You'll need:
- a butter knife
- a serving plate
- measuring cups

Ingredients:

4 plain rice cakes
1/2 cup soft cream cheese
or plain yogurt
1 cup fruit

Yield: 4 pizzas
Time: 15 minutes

Instructions:
Spread the cream cheese or yogurt on the rice cakes. Be sure to cover the whole surface. Wash the fruit and cut into bite-size bits. Place the fruit on the rice cake. Use your imagination. Make a rainbow, spiral, checkerboard or whatever you like. These are a big hit at parties or as an afternoon snack.

Bugs in the Hay Stack

This sweet and wholesome salad is great for lunch served with PB&J Cutouts. This recipe calls for vanilla yogurt but it's also good with lemon or plain yogurt.

You'll need:
- a potato peeler
- a grater
- a medium-size bowl
- measuring cups
- a wooden spoon

Ingredients:

2 cups grated carrots
1/2 cup raisins soaked in 1/2 cup water for 5 minutes
1/2 cup lowfat vanilla yogurt

Yield: 2 servings
Time: 20 minutes

Instructions:
Wash the carrots. Peel them if you like. Using a small grater, grate the carrots into a medium-size bowl. Careful! The grater is sharp and can hurt your fingers. Drain the water from raisins and add to carrots. Measure the yogurt and add it to the carrot-raisin mixture. With a wooden spoon, stir the yogurt into the mixture gently. Serve.

PB&J Cut-Outs

These sandwiches are so much fun to make. Cookie cutters turn a plain sandwich into a work of art. This recipe calls for peanut butter and jelly but you can make cut-outs with just about any type of sandwich.
Try it with cheese or bologna.

You'll need:
- a butter knife
- a Tablespoon
- cookie cutters
- Large cookie cutter the size of a slice of bread, or two small ones. If you don't have cookie cutters, you can also make sandwich circles with the edge of a sturdy plastic glass.

Ingredients:

2 slices of white or wheat bread
peanut butter for one sandwich
2 Tablespoons jelly

Yield: 1 sandwich
Time: 5 minutes

Instructions:

Place the two slices of bread on a work surface. Spread with the peanut butter and jelly.
Put the sandwich together. Use cookie cutters to make your favorite shape.

Tomato and Cheese Sandwiches

This is a delicious way for Fit Kids to get a little bit of extra calcium. It's also good toasted.

You'll need:
- a paring knife
- a butter knife
- a Tablespoon

Ingredients:

2 slices white bread
2 slices cheddar cheese
1 Tablespoon mayonnaise
1 ripe tomato

Yield: 1 sandwich
Time: 10 minutes

Instructions:
Wash the tomato and slice. Place 2 slices of plain or toasted bread on a work surface, side by side. Spread mayonnaise on one slice. Place cheese on the bread without mayonnaise, then top with tomato. Finish the sandwich by placing the second slice of bread or toast on top, mayonnaise side on the tomato. Cut in half. Voila!

Tropical Fruit Salad

Fruit Salad makes a great lunch on a hot summer day. You can add fresh fruit according to your taste. Berries, kiwi or pineapple are good additions to this basic recipe. Add some chopped nuts to make this salad fancy.

You'll need:
- a medium-size serving bowl
- a butter knife
- 2 spoons
- a measuring cup

Ingredients:

1/2 cup shredded coconut
1 orange, peeled and sectioned
1 banana, sliced
1 small can drained pineapple chunks
A handful of seedless grapes

Yield: 1 - 2 serving
Time: 20 minutes

Instructions:
Wash the grapes and set aside. Peel and section the orange and place it in a bowl. Drain the pineapple and add to orange. Slice the banana into the pineapple and orange. Then add grapes. Sprinkle coconut into fruit and gently toss with two spoons until the coconut covers all the fruit. Serve with raisin bread slices or toast.

Tea Party Sandwiches

Sometimes Rosa likes to have her friends over for a special lunch. Each child dresses up in grown-up hats and gloves, necklaces and pretty pins or scarves. Rosa makes fancy place cards for each guest using plain paper and crayons, markers or colored pencils. She sets the table so it looks really nice. Rosa serves fruit juice in teacups along with these sandwiches.

You'll need:
- a butter knife
- a paring knife
- a potato peeler
- measuring cup and spoons

Ingredients:

8 slices of bread
1 cucumber
3/4 cup cream cheese, softened
1 small tomato
4 slices cheddar cheese
2 Tablespoons mayonnaise

Yield: 16 tea sandwiches
Time: 15 minutes

Instructions:

Place the bread slices on the counter or work surface. Spread mayonnaise on 4 pieces of bread and cream cheese on the other 4 pieces. Wash the cucumber and tomato. Peel the cucumber, then slice both the cucumber and tomato. Make the slices thin. Place the cucumber slices on two pieces of bread spread with cream cheese. Top with the other two pieces spread with cream cheese. Place the cheese on the bread topped with mayonnaise.

Add the tomato and top with the remaining mayonnaise coated bread. Cut each sandwich from corner to corner, left to right, into four triangles. Alternate the sandwiches on a serving plate, one tomato and cheese, then one cucumber. Serve with Tropical Fruit Salad made from the recipe in this chapter.

Easy Fit Kids Kabobs

This is a fun and easy recipe that Fit Kids can make for lunch, snacks or special occasions. Use fruit or raw vegetables and add luncheon meat for protein.
We've used fruit for this recipe.

You'll need:
- kabob sticks purchased from the grocery store
- measuring cups
- a paring knife
- a butter knife

Ingredients:

1 cup strawberries
1 cup melon (cantaloupe, watermelon, honeydew)
1 small can pineapple chunks
1/2 cup cubed cheddar cheese
1 large banana cut into 1-inch thick slices
Kabob sticks

In place of fruit, use peeled cucumbers cut into 1-inch thick slices, cherry tomatoes, whole mushrooms, jicama, or any other vegetable firm enough to stay on the stick.
To add luncheon meat, roll the meat slice, cut in half and weave onto the kabob stick between fruit or vegetables.

Yield: 2 - 3 kabobs
Time: 15 minutes

Instructions:

Wash berries, drain pineapple, and peel and cut melon into chunks (or use a large melon baller). Cut cheese into cubes.
Poke the kabob stick through the middle of each ingredient, alternating them as you go.
Slide the fruit down the stick. Be careful, the stick is sharp.
Leave room at the bottom to hold the stick. Arrange on a plate and serve.

48

Smiley Bagels

This recipe calls for vegetables, but you can also make a Smiley Bagel using fruit. Dried, fresh or canned fruit will work just fine. Use canned fruit sweetened in fruit juice instead of sugar. Smiley Bagels are great fun at a party or when friends come for lunch.

You'll need:
- a paring knife
- a potato peeler
- a butter knife
- 3 small bowls

Ingredients

2 - 4 bagels
(flavored or plain)
1 package cream cheese
1 medium carrot cut
onto rounds
1 cucumber sliced
into rounds
1 large bell pepper
cut into thin strips
alfalfa sprouts
(for the hair)

Yield: 2 - 4 bagels
Time: 10 minutes

Instructions:

Place a bagel on a plate and spread with cream cheese using a butter knife. Wash the vegetables and cut them into slices. Set aside in small bowls. Use one bowl for each vegetable. Now everyone gather around and make a smiley face.

BEST FOOT FORWARD

Eating meals together as a family is very important. It's one of Pete and Rosa's favorite things to do. Since families come in all varieties, that means sharing meals with the people you share your life with. They can be people who live in your house, the people who take care of you, your parents, grandparents, brothers and sisters or good friends.

Family MealTime is a good time to share what's going on in your life and catch up on what's going on with the rest of your family. Start with one person and go around the table telling what has happened in your day or what you plan for the day.

American families eat fewer than 20% of their meals together. In many other cultures, meals are shared with family members far more frequently. Food and mealtime is often a celebration. No special occasion, just a time to be happy about life with all its ups and downs. Mealtime celebrates the close ties we have with others and gives us an opportunity to share new eating experiences.

Mealtime should never be hurried and the conversation should be positive and pleasant. Food doesn't digest well if we are upset or angry. You can tell a joke or a funny story at mealtime and make everyone laugh.

BEST FOOT FORWARD

Some people like to start the meal with a prayer. If that's not your custom, each person around the table can take a turn saying one thing they are especially grateful for or happy about. You can also start the meal with a song. Choose a happy family favorite and everyone can sing along.

How the food is presented at the table is also very important.
Presentation means the way food looks. No matter how small or simple the meal, it can be presented in an inviting way.
Here are some suggestions:

Add a sprig of parsley to the serving plate.

Arrange the food in a pattern or design.

Make a flag out of a toothpick and paper to stick in the food on the serving plate or dish.

Make place mats for each person. Draw pictures on a plain sheet of paper or use construction paper if you have it. Include things that are special to that person and put their name on the placemat.

In summer, cut flowers from the garden and put them in a vase, jar or a glass. In the winter when the flowers are sleeping, make some paper flowers using construction paper and glue.

Use mixed up tableware. If you have an assortment of dishes, mix them up to make an interesting table setting.

Fold the napkins in interesting shapes and make napkin rings out of construction paper or tie ribbons around them. Save your wrapping paper from special occasions to make napkin rings.

Fold a strip of wrapping paper or a length of construction paper to make a band and glue or staple into a ring. Slip it over the napkin. If you're out of napkins, folded paper towels work well too.

Napkins should be placed on your lap during meals. Use your napkin throughout the meal to clean food from your face and hands.

Put candles on the table if you have them. Have a grownup light them for you.

And don't forget to look your best for mealtime. Wash your hands and face. Comb your hair. If your clothes are especially dirty from work or play, change into something else. Men and boys – shirts on, please! No hats at the table.

Be sure to thank the cook! If you cooked the meal yourself, be proud of your accomplishment.

Remember that mealtime is a celebration of Y-O-U. No matter how big or small your family, who you call your family, or how simple the meal, you can make it a special occasion to celebrate yourself. Pete and Rosa recommend eating at least one meal each day together as a family.

DINNER

Dinner is special because it's often the only meal of the day that families can share together. Dinner doesn't have to be a fancy affair. The simplest meal can be satisfying. Gather the family around the table, share all of good stuff that happened in your day, sing a song together and be happy for this time you have to share. Read the chapter called Best Foot Forward for some ideas on how to make dinner a special event.

The recipes included in this chapter are fun, nourishing and easy to prepare.

BEFORE WE BEGIN, REMEMBER TO WASH YOUR HANDS! IF THE RECIPE YOU'RE MAKING REQUIRES HELP FROM AN ADULT, BE SURE YOU HAVE DISCUSSED THEIR PARTICIPATION BEFORE YOU START. FOR SAFETY TIPS IN THE KITCHEN, READ THE CLEAN AND SAFE CHAPTER.

Gobbler Cobbler

This recipe is different from most pot pie recipes. The apples and raisins make it sweet. This is a great way to use leftover turkey. To make Hen House Cobbler, use leftover chicken instead of turkey.

You'll need:

- a paring knife
- a medium-size mixing bowl
- a wooden spoon
- measuring cups and spoons
- a pie plate or round baking dish
- oven mitts

Ingredients:

1/2 cup chopped onion
1 Tablespoon butter
2 cans cream of chicken soup
3 cups turkey, cubed
1 large tart apple
1/3 cup raisins
1/2 cup frozen peas
1 teaspoon lemon juice
1/4 teaspoon nutmeg
1 frozen pie crust

Instructions:

Wash the apple. Chop the onion and apple and cut the turkey into bite-size cubes. Put these ingredients into a medium-size mixing bowl. Add the peas. Measure and add the lemon juice, raisins and nutmeg to the mixture. Toss lightly with a wooden spoon to blend. Add the soup right from the can. Don't add water or milk. Mix all ingredients together well. Scoop the filling into a pie plate or other round baking dish. Cover the mixture with the pie crust. Pinch it around the edge so it sticks to the pie plate. Poke a few holes into the top of the pastry with a fork. Bake at 350 degrees for 30 – 45 minutes or until the crust is golden brown. Remove from the oven and cool for 10 minutes before serving.

SALADS ARE GOOD FOR YOU. TO MAKE THEM SPECIAL ADD A FEW TABLESPOONS OF FROZEN VEGETABLES LIKE PEAS OR CORN TO THE SALAD GREENS. REMOVE THE VEGETABLES FROM THE FREEZER, RINSE AND TOSS INTO THE LETTUCE. NO COOKING REQUIRED.

International Smashies

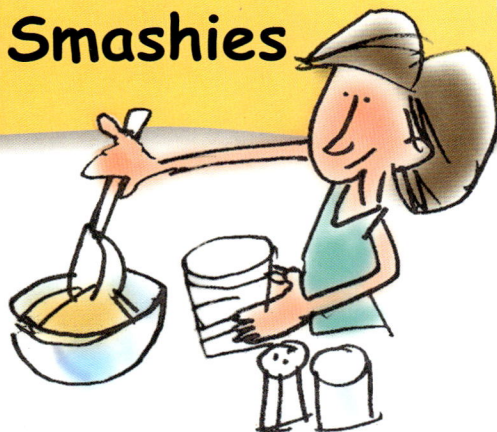

You'll need:

- a medium-size pot
- a hand mixer
- a potato peeler measuring cups and spoons

Ingredients:

packaged instant potatoes or
4 medium potatoes, peeled
1/4 – 1/3 cup reduced fat milk
2 Tablespoons butter
spices to taste

Yield: 4 servings
Time: 20 minutes

Instructions:
Using packaged instant potatoes, make enough potatoes for four people according to package directions. For fresh potatoes: wash the potatoes and peel off the skin. If you have a grownup help peel, it's much faster. Cut the potatoes into pieces, rinse and put them into a pot.
Cover with water.
Cook on medium high until the potatoes are tender when you poke them with a fork.
Drain water.
Be careful. The water is very hot.
Using an electric mixer, mash up the potatoes until they look grainy and the lumps are gone.
Add milk and butter. Whip them until they are soft and smooth.

The chapter called **Spicing it Up** has a listing of spices from different regions around the world. Use the chapter as a guide for spicing up your smashies. For an Italian twist, add a Tablespoon of oregano. You can also add a 1/2 cup grated Parmesan cheese. Go French with a teaspoon of thyme and 2 teaspoons chopped parsley. You can have southwest smashies by adding 2 Tablespoons chopped cilantro (fresh is best) and 1 Tablespoon of mild dried peppers.

Itsy Bitsy Snappy Happy Carrots

These carrots get their "snap" from ginger. You can use fresh or ground ginger depending on what you have on hand. Pete and Rosa like this vegetable dish served with Rosa's Rockin' Meatloaf and International Smashies.

You'll need:
- measuring spoons and cups
- a small grater for fresh ginger
- a microwave-safe bowl
- a wooden spoon
- plastic wrap

Ingredients:

2 Tablespoons butter
1/2 teaspoon ground ginger
1 pound baby carrots
A pinch of salt

Yield: 4 servings
Time: 15 minutes

Instructions:

Use a butter knife to cut 2 Tablespoons butter. Place it in a medium-size microwave-safe bowl. Heat on high for 30 - 45 seconds until the butter is melted. Remove from microwave. Be careful, it will be HOT!
Wash the carrots and set aside. Grate the fresh ginger or measure the ground ginger and add to the butter. Stir to mix. Add the carrots to the butter and mix until they are all coated. Cover with plastic wrap and cook in the microwave on high heat for 10 minutes or until carrots are tender.

Rosa's Rockin' Meatloaf

Rosa's whole family loves this meatloaf and Pete says it really rocks! It's easy to make.

You'll need:
- a pie plate or bread pan
- a medium-size mixing bowl
- measuring spoons and cups
- a wooden spoon
- a paring knife
- oven mitts

Ingredients:

1 pound fresh lean ground beef
6 soda crackers or 1/3 cup uncooked oatmeal
1 egg
1/4 cup lowfat milk
1 small onion
1 glove garlic, minced
1 teaspoon each oregano and basil
1/2 cup catsup

Yield: 4 servings
Prep Time: 20 minutes

Instructions:

In a medium-size mixing bowl, crumble the ground beef. Crush the crackers by placing them in a sandwich bag and hitting them with the heel of your hand. You can also roll over them with a sturdy plastic glass or rolling pin. If using oatmeal, measure it now. Add egg, milk and oatmeal or crackers to the meat and mix together well. You can use your hands to mix this but be sure you wash them well before you handle the mixture. When you're finished squishing it up, wash your hands again. Go to the Clean and Safe chapter for instructions on the proper way to wash your hands. Now, chop the onion and mince the garlic. Add the chopped onion, garlic and spices to the meat mixture. Mix again. If you use your hands, wash them off before and after you mix. Place the meat mixture in a pie plate or bread pan, spreading it out evenly. Pour the catsup on top and spread it around with the back of a wooden spoon. Get it all the way to the edges. Bake at 350 degrees for 1 hour. Serve with International Smashies or a baked potato and Itsy Bitsy Snappy Happy Carrots or your favorite vegetable.

Pete's Famous Spaghetti

Everyone in the neighborhood knows about Pete's spaghetti because it smells so good when it's cooking. This is an easy recipe and a Fit Kids favorite.

You'll need:
- a stock pot or large sauce pan to cook the pasta
- a medium-size pan for sauce
- a can opener
- a wooden spoon
- measuring spoons
- a paring knife
- a colander
- a large serving bowl or deep platter

Ingredients:

1 8-ounce package spaghetti noodles
1 20 – 24 ounce jar pasta sauce
1 medium zucchini
1 small onion
1 clove garlic
1 can mushrooms or
1 cup fresh mushrooms
1 small can sliced olives

Yield: 4 servings
Time: 20 minutes

Instructions:

Fill a saucepan or stockpot with water to about 1 1/2 inches from the top. Place on the stove and turn burner to medium-high. Meanwhile, wash the zucchini and mushrooms if you're using fresh, and chop into bite-size pieces. Chop the onion and garlic. Pour the spaghetti sauce in the medium-size saucepan, add zucchini, onion and garlic, and mushrooms if you're using fresh. Turn burner to medium-high. When it starts to bubble, stir and reduce heat to low. Drain olives and the canned mushrooms if you aren't using fresh. Add to the sauce and stir. When the water begins to boil in the other pot, add the pasta and 1 Tablespoon cooking oil. Stir it every once in a while so the pasta doesn't stick together. When the pasta is soft, drain it into a colander.
Get help with this step. The water is very hot. Pour the drained pasta into a large bowl and cover it with the sauce.
Toss and serve immediately.

Rosa's Saturday BaHoDi

Rosa got this recipe from a very important chef who lives in New York. It seems that when he was going to cooking school to learn to be a very important chef, his class had an assignment every Saturday:

CLEAN OUT THE REFRIGERATOR!

The students had to prepare a meal using all the leftover bits and pieces from the week's cooking. They called it Back House Dish or BaHoDi for short. BaHoDi is simple to make. Look at what's leftover in your refrigerator. There's probably a piece of chicken or maybe some meatloaf.

Be sure that cooked meats are not more than 3 or 4 days old. No leftovers used in this dish should be more than a week old. Check the cupboard to see what canned vegetables you have if there aren't any leftover veggies. What else have you got? Maybe some leftover rice. How about noodles or potato smashies? The important thing is the spice.

Will you make this a southwestern dish by adding some chili peppers? Rice and chicken can easily become an oriental dish with a few simple vegetables like shredded cabbage, onion, a stalk or two of celery, and just the right spice. Look at the chapter called Spicing It Up to decide what kind of spin you want to put on your BaHoDi.

Since most of the ingredients will already be cooked, you can mix them up in a mixing bowl, add spices and pour into a microwave-safe dish. Cook in the microwave for 15 - 20 minutes, depending on how much food. You have a splendid meal that's tasty and very creative. Who knows? Maybe one day you'll be a very important chef!

Cold Veggie Pizza

A super Fit Kids meal you can make in a hurry. Rosa loves to make these pizzas for her friends. You can add additional vegetables to suit your taste.

You'll need:
- a rolling pin
- a cookie sheet or pizza pan
- a paring knife
- a medium-size bowl
- a cheese grater
- oven mitts

Ingredients:

1 tube refrigerated crescent roll dough
1/2 cup grated mozzarella cheese
2 Tablespoons Italian salad dressing
1/2 cup chopped broccoli
1/4 cup chopped carrots
1/2 cup chopped cucumbers
1/2 cup chopped tomato

Yield: 1 pizza
Time: 20 minutes

Instructions:
Roll the crescent dough out onto a baking sheet or round pizza pan.
Turn the oven to 375 degrees. Bake the dough for 10-12 minutes until golden brown. Cool.
Chop the vegetables into small pieces and toss with salad dressing in a medium-size bowl.
Spread the vegetable mixture over the dough all the way to the edges.
Sprinkle with grated mozzarella cheese. Serve.

Pasta Pinwheels

You can have lots of Fit Kids fun serving these Pasta Pinwheels. They're very nutritious!

You'll need:
- a large pot or stockpot for the pasta
- measuring cups and spoons
- a cheese grater
- a butter knife
- a colander
- a large mixing bowl
- a medium-size baking dish
- oven mitts

Ingredients:

1 10-ounce package frozen spinach
1 cup reduced fat ricotta cheese
6 ounces mozzarella cheese, shredded
1 teaspoon Italian seasoning
8 lasagna noodles
2 cups pasta sauce

Yield: 8 pinwheels
Time: 45 minutes

Instructions:
Cook the lasagna noodles according to instructions on the box. When the pasta is done, drain and rinse with cold water. Be very careful! Set aside to cool. Cook the spinach according to package directions. When it's done, drain. Press on the spinach in the colander to get all the water out. Place the cooked and drained spinach in a large bowl. Measure the ricotta cheese and Italian seasoning and add to the spinach. Mix well. Grate the mozzarella and add to the spinach mixture. Mix this well too. Lay the cooked lasagna noodles on the counter or other work surface. Divide the cheese mixture into 8 portions. Spread the cheese mixture on each noodle, end to end, and roll them up. Place the pinwheels in a baking dish, pinwheel facing up. Cover with the pasta sauce. Turn the oven to 350 degrees and bake for 30 minutes. Cool slightly before serving.

Yankee Doodle Dogs

You can turn plain old macaroni and cheese into a hearty Fit Kids meal with this easy recipe.

You'll need:
- a sauce pan
- measuring cups
- a butter knife
- a microwave-safe plate
- a small microwave-safe bowl
- plastic wrap

Ingredients:

1 package macaroni and cheese
4 hot dogs
1 cup frozen peas, optional

Yield: 4 servings
Time: 20 minutes

Instructions:

Prepare macaroni and cheese according to instructions on the box.
Place the hot dogs on a microwave-safe plate and heat for 1 1/2 minutes. When they are done, remove them from the microwave, cool slightly then cut into bite-size pieces with the butter knife.
Add the hot dogs to the macaroni and stir. Cook peas in microwave-safe bowl covered with plastic wrap for two minutes. Add cooked peas now and stir again. It's yummy.

Do It Yourself Veggie Soup

Pete likes to experiment so sometimes he adds different vegetables from the ones we've listed here. This recipe is good with a sandwich on the side.

COME AND GET IT!!!

You'll need:
- a medium-size saucepan
- a can opener
- measuring cups

Ingredients:

1/4 cup dehydrated onion
1 cup chicken broth
1 16-ounce can chopped tomatoes
1 8 ounce can green beans
1 can corn

Yield: 6 servings
Time: 20 minutes

Instructions:
Place a saucepan on the stove.
Add the broth and dehydrated onion.
Turn the burner to medium-high.
Open cans and drain the liquid from the beans and corn but not the tomatoes.
Add these ingredients to the pan. Stir.
Reduce heat to medium-low and cook until completely heated. Serve with your favorite sandwich.

Personal Pitas

It's fun to make this sandwich with a friend. This recipe makes two pitas. To serve four, double the ingredients.

You'll need:
- a butter knife
- 5 small bowls (one should be microwave-safe)
- a cheese grater
- oven mitts
- measuring cups

Ingredients:

2 pitas cut in half
1 cup lettuce shredded or torn
1 chopped tomato
1/2 cup canned black beans
1/2 cup mild salsa
3/4 cup grated cheddar cheese

Yield: 2 pitas
Time: 10 minutes

Instructions:
Drain the liquid from the black beans. Empty into microwave-safe bowl and heat in microwave on high for 3 minutes. Remove and set aside. Tear or shred lettuce into small pieces, and slice the tomato. Put them in individual bowls and set aside. Grate the cheese into a small bowl. Set aside. Set one pita pocket on each plate and open. Now fill the pockets with the ingredients and you're ready to eat.

Baked "Fried" Chicken

This is a fun and healthy way to have fried chicken without all the grease. Serve it for a Fit Kids family get-together.

Instructions:

Place the crackers in a re-sealable plastic bag and crush them using the heel of your hand, a rolling pin or a heavy plastic glass. Open the bag and add the flour, salt and pepper. Close the bag and shake it up to mix the ingredients.

In a shallow dish, add the egg and milk and beat with a fork or wire whisk.

Spray a baking dish with the cooking spray until the bottom is coated. Wash the chicken off with warm water and pat dry with clean paper towels. Be sure to throw the paper towels away immediately. Don't use them for anything else. Coat the chicken pieces in the egg mixture, one piece at a time, and then place the chicken in the plastic bag with the cracker mixture. Do this one piece at a time. Shake until the chicken piece is coated well. Remove and place it in the baking dish. Bake at 350 degrees for 30 – 45 minutes until chicken is done. Serve with international smashies and a vegetable. Try serving this cold with baked beans and coleslaw for a picnic.

You'll need:
- a re-sealable plastic food bag
- a pie plate or other shallow dish
- a shallow baking dish
- measuring spoons
- a fork or wire whisk
- oven mitts

Ingredients:

20 soda crackers
3 Tablespoons flour
1/2 teaspoon garlic salt
1/2 teaspoon pepper
1 egg
1 Tablespoon milk
cooking spray
4 boneless, skinless chicken breasts

Yield: 4 servings
Time: 45 minutes

Quesadilla Stacker

Pete makes these stackers for dinner on nights when he's home alone. His mom grates the cheese and chops the veggies for him before she goes to work and he's very careful using the microwave. This recipe makes one stacker but you can make more to feed the whole family. Just multiply the ingredients by the number of people you will be serving.

You'll need:
- measuring cups
- a paring knife
- a medium-size mixing bowl
- a cheese grater
- a microwave-safe plate
- oven mitts

Ingredients:

3 flour tortillas
1 small green pepper, chopped
1 small onion, chopped
1/2 cup salsa
1/2 cup broccoli, chopped
1/2 cup cauliflower, chopped
1 cup refried beans
1 cup cheddar cheese, shredded

Yield: 1 stacker
Time: 15 minutes

Instructions:
Wash all the vegetables and chop them into small pieces. Place them in a bowl and set aside. Grate the cheese and set it aside. Measure the refried beans and salsa and set aside. Place 1 tortilla on a microwave safe plate.
Spread half the refried beans on the tortilla and top with half the salsa. Sprinkle 1/3 of the cheese on top.
Cover with another tortilla. Put the vegetable mixture on top of the second tortilla and add another 1/3 of the cheese. Place another tortilla on top and add the rest of the refried beans and salsa. Sprinkle with remaining cheese. Heat in the microwave on high for 3 minutes or until cheese is melted. Be careful when you take it out. Cheese is very hot when it's melted.

PETE DOESN'T ALWAYS LIKE SALAD DRESSING. OH, WHAT TO DO? TRY TOSSING THE SALAD GREENS IN 1/4 CUP ORANGE JUICE INSTEAD OF SALAD DRESSING.

SPICING IT UP

Did you ever wonder why food tastes different at someone else's house? When parents and grandparents come from other parts of the world they bring the wonderful tradition of their native foods with them to America.

Some of these native foods are quite different from the typical American food many of us find on our table. And sometimes, by adding native spices to what we know as typical American food, or changing the way the food is cooked, the taste becomes unique. These differences are what make the food and the people so special.

Spices that come from different regions of the world influence the food. Most of these spices are available in American grocery stores.

Start with a small quantity of the spice at first so you don't overwhelm the food.

Italian and French cooks use bay leaf, parsley, oregano, basil, chervil, rosemary, fennel, thyme, dill, marjoram, tarragon, garlic, sage and caraway. These spices are used on vegetables, meat, poultry and fish, in sauces and even desserts.

67

Southwestern, Mexican and Latin cooks use allspice, bay leaf, cumin, cilantro, chili powder, cinnamon, garlic, oregano, dried peppers and dried chiles and fresh hot peppers.

Pete's Special Southwest Sandwich is simple to make. Season 1/2 pound ground beef with 1 teaspoon each of cumin, minced garlic and chopped cilantro. Cook the beef in a skillet with the spices. When the beef is done, add 1 Tablespoon prepared chili sauce to the meat mixture. Spread on a warm flour tortilla. Roll the tortilla and, with fold down on the plate, slice into bite-size roll-ups. Serve with a sliced pear, apple or peach for a tasty lunch.

On cold winter days, Pete and Rosa make festive hot cocoa. Make cocoa according to the package directions. Add 1/8 teaspoon cinnamon to the beverage and stir. Top with whipped cream if you have it on hand and sprinkle a dash of cinnamon on top.

Rosa suggests these simple recipes using French and Italian spices. For a tasty Italian dish, drain and rinse one 15-ounce can of white northern beans and place in a medium-size bowl. Toss the beans with 2 teaspoons olive oil, 2 Tablespoons fresh or dried oregano, a teaspoon of basil and a teaspoon of minced garlic. Heat in the microwave for 3 - 4 minutes and serve as a side dish with meat and a leafy green vegetable. Rosa also likes them served cold on a bed of lettuce with sliced tomatoes. Garnish the salad with olives.

French Broiled Tomatoes are easy to make too. Cut a fresh tomato in half, scrape out the seeds and set the tomato aside.
Mix a crushed garlic clove, 1/2 teaspoon of crushed rosemary and 1 teaspoon olive oil into a small bowl and stir together.
Add a teaspoon of bread crumbs to the oil and spices and stir again. Spoon into tomato halves. Bake in a shallow baking dish on 350 for 10 - 15 minutes.

Simple Spaghetti is an easy Italian recipe. Slice 2 fresh tomatoes and arrange on a cookie sheet. Sprinkle with 1Tablespoon fresh or dried oregano, 1 Tablespoon fresh or dried basil, 1 Tablespoon olive oil, and 1 clove minced garlic. Top with 1/2 cup grated Parmesan cheese. Broil in the oven on the top shelf for 5 minutes or until the cheese melts. Serve over cooked pasta.

Spicing Tips

Indian and Middle Eastern food is seasoned with cardamom, chervil, cilantro, marjoram, mint, nutmeg, parsley, pepper, saffron, turmeric and mustard seed.

Curry paste and curry powder can be used in many dishes. Some varieties are hot and others are mild.

Oriental or Asian cooking includes ginger, garlic, pepper, cilantro, mint, mustard, cumin and parsley. You can also add sesame seeds to oriental cooking. Fresh ginger is good too. Try it on vegetables, chicken and in rice.

Some cultures use a combination of spices that originated when one group of people relocated to another part of the world. They added that regions' spices to their own. For example, traditional African American cooks may incorporate spices and foods from the southern part of the United States, from their native Africa, and from the various regions where they may have lived when they left Africa.

For a simple sandwich try cutting leftover chicken pieces into bite-size cubes. You'll need about a cup of cubed chicken. Put the chicken in a bowl and add 1/4 cup raisins, 3/4 to 1-teaspoon mild curry powder and enough mayonnaise to coat the mixture. Put the mixture in a pita pocket or between two slices of your favorite bread. Delicious!

Pastas Around the World

Every culture has a pasta all its own. Pasta is a good source of carbohydrate, fiber and sometimes protein.
The Chinese serve rice noodles. Italians use egg noodle pasta like rotini or shells.

Here are some Fit Kids tips for cooking pasta:

You will need adult supervision when cooking pasta. It cooks in boiling water, which can splash out of the pan and burn you. The steam from the water is hot. Always be careful when you cook pasta.

The water for pasta should be brought to a boil and kept at a rapid boil until the pasta is done. Pasta takes from 5 - 20 minutes to cook depending on how much and what kind you're making.

Pasta must be drained before you serve it. That means getting all the boiling water out of the pan. This is usually done by pouring the pasta and water into a colander that has holes in the bottom so the water can drain. Kids should not attempt this on their own.

Draining the pasta stops the cooking. When the pasta will be cooked again, in lasagna or a baked dish, rinse it in cold water after cooking. Generally, one pound of pasta feeds four people as a main course.

PLUNK 'N' GO MEALS

Plunk 'N' Go meals are meals made in a hurry, generally using prepared foods rather than fresh. Sometimes these recipes cook for several hours but they don't require a lot of work to put them together. Just plunk the ingredients into a pot and go about your business.

Down in the Dumplings

Sometimes, when Pete and Rosa are down in the dumps, nothing works better to boost their spirits than a healthy meal. This is very easy to make. It will fill your tummy and warm your heart.

You'll need:
- a can opener
- a large sauce pan with a lid

Ingredients:

1 large can (24 – 32-ounces) homestyle chicken noodle or chicken vegetable soup. You'll want the kind that you don't dilute with water.
1 package buttermilk biscuits

Yield: 2 servings
Prep time: 10 minutes

Instructions:

Open soup and pour into sauce pan. Heat on medium-high until it starts to bubble. Open the biscuits and place them on top of the soup. Reduce heat to low. Cook uncovered for 10 minutes. Cover and cook for an another 10 minutes or until the dumplings are cooked through.

Creamy Corn Soup

A quick and easy soup to warm your tummy on a cold day. Creamy Corn Soup is one of Rosa's favorites.

COME AND GET IT!!!

You'll need:
- a can opener
- a medium-size pan or Dutch oven
- a paring knife
- a wooden spoon
- measuring cups and spoons
- a butter knife

Ingredients:

2 Tablespoons butter
1 large green pepper, chopped
1 medium onion, chopped
1 14 ounce can diced tomatoes in juice
2 cups water
2 14 ounce cans cream style corn
1 16 ounce package frozen corn
1 cup whole milk or half and half
1 teaspoon oregano

Yield: 6 servings
PrepTime: 20 minutes

Instructions:
Melt the butter in a large pan or Dutch oven over medium heat. Add chopped onion and green pepper. Cook, stirring gently until the onion is transparent. Add canned tomatoes, canned corn, water, milk or half and half and stir. Add frozen corn and oregano. Stir until all ingredients are well blended. Cook over medium heat for 15 minutes. Reduce to simmer. Cover and cook for 30 – 40 minutes.

Stone Soup

This recipe is inspired by a classic story about a town full of people who came together over a pot of soup. It seems that each person in the town was quite selfish and hoarded what few vegetables they had, unwilling to share with their neighbors. A stranger came to town and set up a large soup pot over a fire, right in the middle of the town square. He filled it with water and a few stones.

When people passed by and asked him what he was doing, the stranger said he was making stone soup and offered each person a taste. Everyone tasted the soup and made a similar comment: the soup was good but it needed a little something. And each one who tasted the bland soup decided they could spare a little something – a carrot here, a turnip there, some corn, and a few potatoes.

Pretty soon the soup was brimming with all kinds of good things and it was delicious. The town's people got together and enjoyed the soup they had all made by sharing a little of what they each had.

Pete and Rosa don't recommend starting the soup with water and stones but this is a good recipe. You can have a stone soup party and ask each guest to bring one item. Everyone can help prepare the soup and hang out or play games while it cooks.

You'll need:

- a stock pot or large pan
- measuring cups
- a paring knife

Ingredients:

6 cups water
12 bouillon cubes
1 package frozen corn
2 potatoes, peeled and diced
3 carrots, peeled and sliced
1/2 cup diced celery
1/2 cup chopped onion

Yield: 6 servings
PrepTime: about 10 minutes

Instructions:

Add the bouillon cubes and water to a large stockpot. Bring to a boil then reduce heat to medium-low. Wash the vegetables and, if you need to, get help peeling and chopping them. Add them to the pot. Add the frozen corn, stir and cover. Cook on medium-low for 1 1/2 hours or until the potatoes and carrots are soft when poked with a fork. Serve in soup bowls with slices of buttered bread.

74

Little Trees in the Hen House

This is a quick dinner favorite but it can also be served for breakfast with muffins and jam.

You'll need:
- a cheese grater
- a paring knife
- a wire whisk or fork
- a wooden spoon
- measuring cups and spoons
- a colander
- a medium-size mixing bowl
- a slow cooker or baking dish
- oven mitts

Ingredients:

1 8 ounce carton lowfat cottage cheese
1 10-ounce package frozen broccoli or
1 1/2 cups fresh broccoli, chopped
1/2 cup shredded cheddar cheese
2 eggs, beaten
4 teaspoons flour
1 Tablespoon chopped onion
1 Tablespoon butter

Yield: 2 - 3 servings
Prep Time: 15 minutes

Instructions:

This recipe can be baked in the oven or cooked in a slow cooker.
Using the butter, grease the bottom and sides of the baking dish or slow cooker. Crack the eggs in a medium size bowl and beat with a fork until they are creamy yellow and fluffy. Using a colander, rinse the frozen broccoli under warm water. Shake all the extra water out. Set aside. For fresh broccoli, get help cooking this in the microwave. Add all the remaining ingredients to the eggs. Mix well. Add the broccoli and mix again. Pour the mixture into the slow cooker and cook at least 1 hour or until the eggs are set.

USE YOUR IMAGINATION TO MAKE YOUR OWN PLUNK 'N' GO MEALS.

Tummy Tempting Tuna Casserole

A great dinner for the whole family. For this recipe, Pete and Rosa like wide egg noodles but you can use whatever kind of noodles you have on hand.

You'll need:
- a can opener
- a colander
- a medium-size mixing bowl
- a large baking dish
- stock pot or a large sauce pan
- oven mitts

Ingredients:

1 8-ounce package noodles
2 cans tuna, drained
1 can cream of mushroom soup
1/2 cup corn cereal or cracker crumbs, crushed

Yield: 6 servings
Time: 20 minutes

Instructions:
In a large pot, boil the water for the noodles. Open the tuna and drain. Be careful of the sharp edges on the cans. Set aside. Open the soup. When the water is boiling, add the noodles and cook as directed on the package. When the noodles are done, get help draining them into a colander. The steam will be very hot so don't try this alone. Pour the noodles into a large baking dish.
Put the drained tuna and soup into the mixing bowl and mix it up. Spread the mixture on top of the noodles. Be sure to cover all of them. Sprinkle crumbs on top. Bake at 350 degrees for 30 minutes until the top is brown. Remove from the oven carefully. It will be very hot. Set it on the table on a heat resistant trivet or pot holder. Serve immediately.

Slow as a Donkey Casserole

This recipe can be made in a crock-pot or in a Dutch oven on the stovetop. It cooks for a long time on very low heat. Pete and Rosa make this for their whole family.

You'll need:
- a can opener
- measuring cup and spoons
- a wooden spoon
- a crock pot or Dutch oven
- a paring knife

Ingredients:

2 cans red beans
1 can corn
1 pound lean ground beef
1 cup cheddar cheese
1 can olives
1 can or package tamales
1 teaspoon chili powder
1 teaspoon cumin

Yield: about 8 servings
PrepTime: about 10 minutes

Instructions:

Crumble the uncooked ground beef into a crock pot or Dutch oven. Wash your hands before and after you handle the meat. Open the tamales and remove the paper wrappers. If using canned, break or cut them into 1-inch pieces and place into the pot. Open the remaining cans, drain liquid and add to the contents to the pot. Cut the cheddar cheese into cubes and add to the pot.

Now measure the spices and sprinkle on top of the mound of ingredients. Stir gently two or three times. Cover. If using a crock pot, turn the heat to high for 30 minutes. After 30 minutes reduce to lowest heat and cook for 4 hours or longer. Stir once each hour to blend ingredients. If cooking on the stovetop, start with medium heat and reduce to low as soon as the meat begins to cook. Stir every hour. Cook on the stovetop for 2 – 3 hours. The longer it cooks, the better it tastes. Serve in chili bowls.

Snacks

Snacks are an important part of the day for kids. Eating healthy snacks everyday is a good way to get the right number of servings of all of theimportant foods in the food pyramid. At snack time, it's best to avoid "junk" food. Instead, eat wholesome foods that have healthy nutrients to fuel your body. These recipes let you show off your creativity.

BEFORE WE BEGIN, REMEMBER TO WASH YOUR HANDS! IF THE RECIPE YOU'RE MAKING REQUIRES HELP FROM AN ADULT, BE SURE YOU HAVE DISCUSSED THEIR PARTICIPATION BEFORE YOU START. FOR SAFETY TIPS IN THE KITCHEN, READ THE CLEAN AND SAFE CHAPTER.

Cheese Bugs

Edible bugs. Wow! This recipe is so easy and you don't need any grownup help.

You'll need:
- a serving plate

Ingredients:

1 one ounce package string cheese
7 pretzel sticks

Yield: 1 cheese bug
Time: 5 minutes

Instructions:
Unwrap the cheese and place it on the plate. Press 3 pretzel sticks into each side of the string cheese to make the bug legs. Break the last pretzel stick in half and put those pieces in the end of the string cheese, poking up, to make feelers.

Fruit Smoothie

Smoothies are really delicious. They make a great snack or a wholesome breakfast.

You'll need:
• a blender
• 2 large glasses
• measuring cups
• a butter knife

Ingredients:
1/3 cup vanilla yogurt
1 cup raspberries
or blueberries
1 ripe banana
1 cup unsweetened
apple juice
2 ice cubes

Yield: 1 smoothie
Time: 10 minutes

Instructions:
Measure the yogurt and apple juice into the blender. Wash the berries and set on a paper towel to drain. Peel the banana and cut into 3 or 4 pieces. Add all ingredients to the blender. Add 2 ice cubes. Put the lid on the blender. Make sure it's on tight. Blend until smooth. Pour into 1 large or 2 small glasses.

Fruit with Yogurt

This recipe is very healthy because it's made with fresh fruit. It's an excellent Fit Kids snack!

You'll need:
• measuring cups
• a butter knife
• a small mixing bowl
• a spoon
Ingredients:

1/2 cup strawberries
1 small banana, sliced
1/2 cup seedless grapes
1 cup plain, vanilla or lemon
flavored yogurt

Yield: 2 servings
Time: 10 minutes

Instructions:
Spoon the yogurt into a small bowl. Wash the grapes and berries. Cut the berries and banana into bite-size pieces with a butter knife. Add the fruit to the yogurt. Spoon into individual serving bowls.

Spider Bites

We all need to watch out for spiders but these cute little critters are harmless. It's no surprise that Pete loves this snack treat. These are easy to make.

You'll need:
- a butter knife
- a plate
- measuring spoons

Ingredients:

4 round crackers
2 Tablespoons cheese spread or peanut butter
8 pretzel sticks
4 raisins

Yield: 2 spiders
Time: 5 minutes

Instructions:
Place the crackers on a plate and spread with cheese spread or peanut butter using a butter knife. Put the crackers together to make 2 cracker sandwiches. Break the pretzel sticks in half so you have 16 equal sized pieces (8 legs for each spider.) Insert eight pieces of the pretzel sticks into the filling of each cracker sandwich to make eight legs. Using a little bit of filling, set 2 raisins on top the cracker sandwiches to make eyes.

Ants on a Log

Besides his fascination with spiders, Pete loves ants. He can spend hours watching them work. This is one of his favorite recipes.

You'll need:
- a paring knife
- a butter knife
- a serving plate

Ingredients:
2 celery stocks
2 Tablespoons peanut butter
8 raisins

Yield: 2 logs
Time: 5 minutes

Instructions:
Wash the celery and cut the ends off. Get help if you're too little to use knives. Spread the peanut butter into the center of the celery from end to end. Place 4 raisins on each "log". If you place them in a row it will look like the ants are marching.

Apple Salsa and Cinna-chips

With this recipe you can make your own chips and salsa. It's very easy and lots of fun.

You'll need:
- a paring knife
- a small bowl
- measuring cups and spoons
- a cookie sheet
- oven mitts

Ingredients:

Salsa:
1 medium apple, chopped
1 cup strawberries
2 kiwi fruit, peeled and chopped
1 small orange
3 Tablespoons apple jelly

Chips:
8 flour tortillas
1 Tablespoon water
1/4 cup honey
2 teaspoons cinnamon

Yield: 6 servings
Time: 20 minutes

Instructions:

Wash the fruit. Chop the apple and cut the tops off the strawberries. Place them in a bowl. Grate the orange peel into the fruit then cut the orange in half and squeeze the juice onto the fruit. Add the apple jelly which has been warmed to room temperature. Stir it all together and set it aside. Now it's time to make the chips. Measure and mix the cinnamon and honey together in a small bowl. Set aside. Set the tortillas on the counter or work surface and brush them lightly with the water. Drizzle the honey and cinnamon over the tortillas. Cut each tortilla into 8 triangles and place on a cookie sheet. Bake in a 400 degree oven for 7 – 10 minutes until they are lightly brown.
Remove from the oven and let cool. Serve with the salsa.

Vegetable Salsa Burritos

A healthy Fit Kids snack. Pete and Rosa love making this nutritious salsa to wrap up in tortillas. Served with a smoothie, this could be a whole meal.

You'll need:
- a paring knife
- a small mixing bowl
- measuring spoons
- a serving plate

Ingredients:

1 large tomato
1 small cucumber
1 small avocado
1 Tablespoon lemon juice
1 Tablespoon mayonnaise
pinch of salt and pepper
4 small tortillas

Yield: 4 burritos
Time: 15 minutes

Instructions:
Wash the vegetables and chop them into small pieces. Place them into a small bowl. Measure and add the lemon juice. Add a pinch of salt and pepper. Stir vegetables and seasoning together. Measure the mayonnaise and add that too. Mix gently. Place a tortilla on a plate and put about 1/4 cup of the vegetable salsa in a line down the center. Roll it up. Do the same with the rest of the tortillas.

Happy Trails Mix

This is a fun snack to take on long trips or into the backyard to play. You can share this treat with your friends.

You'll need:
- measuring cups
- a paring knife
- a resealable plastic food storage bag

Ingredients:

2 cups dry cereal like puffed rice or wheat, Kix or Chex
1 cup peanuts
1/2 cup chopped dried fruit
1/2 cup raisins

Yield: 5 cups
Time: 5 minutes

Instructions:
Chop the dried fruit. Combine all the ingredients in a large resealable plastic bag or covered container and seal. Shake to mix ingredients.

SNACK TIME IS A GOOD TIME TO USE YOUR IMAGINATION. YOU CAN CREATE ALL KINDS OF FUN AND HEALTHY SNACK FOODS. USE THE RECIPES IN THIS CHAPTER AS A GUIDE FOR MAKING WHOLESOME FIT KIDS TREATS TO ENJOY BETWEEN MEALS.

Watermelon Split

Instead of plain old bananas and ice cream, this healthy recipe calls for watermelon and berries. Use yogurt instead of ice cream. It's is a big hit with Fit Kids.

You'll need:
- a butter knife
- an ice cream scoop
- 4 banana split dishes or bowls
- measuring cups

Ingredients:
1 banana
4 scoops watermelon
1 cup blueberries
1 cup low fat vanilla yogurt
1/2 cup granola

Yield: 4 servings
Time: 10 minutes

Instructions:
Wash the berries and set them aside to drain.
Peel the banana lengthwise and then in half so you have four pieces.
Place a piece of banana in each of 4 small dishes.
Use an ice cream scoop to scoop out 4 gobs of watermelon and place one in each dish.
Add blueberries on top of the watermelon, then add a scoop of yogurt.
Sprinkle the top of each Watermelon Split with granola.

NEED A SNACK IN A HURRY? INSTEAD OF GRABBING A SWEET, TRY AN APPLE OR OTHER FRESH FRUIT, CARROT AND CELERY STICKS, PRETZELS, CHEESE AND CRACKERS, A WHOLE FRESH TOMATO, OR NATURAL APPLESAUCE. THESE ARE WHOLESOME TREATS THAT WILL STICK TO YOUR RIBS AND HELP YOU STAY HEALTHY.

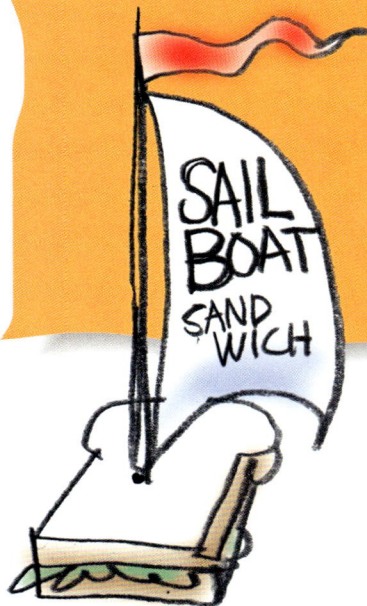

Sailboat Sandwiches

Make up a fun story to go along with these Fit Kids Sailboat Sandwiches. Are you off the coast of Maine in the United States or in a foreign country? Pete likes to imagine he's on a tropical island in search of coconuts along the shore. Rosa pretends her sailboat is whisking her on the sea to an exotic land.

Instructions:

Open the can of tuna and drain the liquid. In a small bowl, add tuna and mayonnaise. Mix well.
Slice the tops off of the dinner rolls and scoop out the centers. Fill the rolls with the tuna salad.
With a butter knife, cut the cheese slices into triangles.
Place a toothpick into each triangle to make a sail and attach to "boat".

You'll need:
- a small mixing bowl
- measuring spoons
- a butter knife
- toothpicks

Ingredients:

1 can tuna
3 Tablespoons mayonnaise
3-4 dinner rolls
4 slices cheddar cheese

Yield: 3 to 4 boats
Time: 10 minutes

Nachos

Pete and Rosa like nachos instead of plain chips. Munch on these treats with some carrots and celery for a great after school snack.

You'll need:
- a cheese grater
- a microwave-safe plate
- a measuring cup
- oven mitts

Ingredients:

2 cups corn tortilla chips
1 cup grated cheddar cheese

Yield: 1 to 2 servings
Time: 10 minutes

Instructions:

Place 1 cup tortilla chips on a microwave-safe plate. Grate the cheese. It's okay to use packaged cheese that's already grated. Sprinkle 1/2 of the cheese over the top of the tortilla chips. Toss a little with your CLEAN hands. Add the remaining cup of tortilla chips and top with cheese. Toss lightly with your hands. Place the plate into the microwave and heat on high for 2 minutes. They may need more time depending on your microwave. When the cheese is melted, take them out and eat. Be careful. Cheese is very hot when it's melted. Cool before eating.

SWEET TREATS

Sometimes we just want a sweet treat and nothing else will do. Sweets can actually be good for us and they can supply some of the important nutrients we need during the day. It's important to choose them wisely.

Before you start munching on a candy bar or pop the top off a soda, think about making one of these sweet treat recipes. These are some of Pete and Rosa's favorite sweet treats.

BEFORE WE BEGIN, REMEMBER TO WASH YOUR HANDS! IF THE RECIPE YOU'RE MAKING REQUIRES HELP FROM AN ADULT, BE SURE YOU HAVE DISCUSSED THEIR PARTICIPATION BEFORE YOU START. FOR SAFETY TIPS IN THE KITCHEN, READ THE CLEAN AND SAFE CHAPTER.

Brown Cow Pops

This recipe doesn't require any help from a grownup. You'll need to plan ahead for this treat because it has to stay in the freezer for several hours.

You'll need:
- measuring cups and spoons
- 6 3-ounce paper drinking cups
- 6 Popsicle sticks
- a blender

Ingredients:

1 cup chocolate milk
1 ripe banana
1 teaspoon vanilla
2 Tablespoons chocolate syrup

Yield: 6 pops
Time: 5 minutes

Instructions:
Measure the ingredients and put them into the blender. Put the lid on tight and blend the for one minute. Pour into cups and cover each cup with aluminum foil. Poke a popsicle stick through the foil and into the mixture. Freeze. When pops are frozen, remove from freezer and carefully dip them in warm water just up to the cup rim. Leave 3 –4 seconds. The cup should slide off easily.

Rice Pudding

Pete and Rosa like to make this treat on cold winter days but it's good anytime of year. Rice pudding is easy to make and really yummy!

You'll need:
- a small saucepan and lid
- a large mixing bowl
- a butter knife
- measuring cups and spoons
- a baking dish
- oven mitts

Ingredients:

2 cups instant white rice, cooked
1 1/3 cups milk
pinch of salt
1/2 cup fruit-sweetened jam or 1/3 cup fruit juice concentrate
1 Tablespoon butter or cooking spray
3 eggs
1/3 cup raisins

Yield: 6 servings
PrepTime: about 15 minutes

Instructions:

In a saucepan, cook the instant rice according to instructions on the package.
When it's done, pour the rice into a large mixing bowl.
Cool for a few minutes. Add the remaining ingredients and mix well.
Grease a large baking dish with the butter or coat with cooking spray. Pour the mixture into the dish.
Place in a 325 degree preheated oven and bake 45 minutes or until set. When it is done, remove from oven and let cool.

INSTEAD OF REACHING FOR A CANDY BAR OR PREPACKAGED TREAT, TRY SOME FRESH OR DRIED FRUIT . YOU'LL GET SOME OF THE IMPORTANT NUTRIENTS YOUR BODY NEEDS TO STAY HEALTHY, AND FRUIT IS ALWAYS TASTY.

Strawberry Shortcake

This is a quick and easy dessert and it's better for you than traditional strawberry shortcake.

You'll need:
- a cookie sheet
- measuring cups
- a butter knife
- a paring knife
- oven mitts

Ingredients:

1 tube biscuits, buttermilk or plain
1 cup strawberries
1 cup vanilla or strawberry yogurt

Yield: 4 servings
Time: 10 minutes

Instructions:
Bake the biscuits according to package directions. When they are cool, cut 4 biscuits in half and place them side by side on a serving plate with the inside facing up. Wash the strawberries and remove tops. Place a handful of strawberries on the biscuits. Top with a big scoop of yogurt.

FOR A COOL SWEET TREAT, ROSA FREEZES FRUIT JUICE IN ICE TRAYS IN THE FREEZER. WHEN THE ICE IS FROZEN SOLID, SHE TOSSES THE CUBES IN THE BLENDER AND CRUSHES THEM JUST A LITTLE (NOT TOO MUCH OR IT WILL BE MUSH) THEN POURS THE ICY JUICE INTO A GLASS FOR A WHOLESOME HOMEMADE SNOWCONE.

Apple Squares

Fit Kids will enjoy this yummy apple snack. Plan ahead because you bake this in the oven and it has to cool before you can eat it.

You'll need:
- a large mixing bowl
- measuring cups and spoons
- a paring knife
- a wooden spoon
- a large baking dish
- oven mitts

Ingredients:

2 1/2 cups all-purpose flour
2/3 cups frozen apple juice concentrate
2 eggs
1/2 cup natural applesauce
1/4 cup canola oil
1 teaspoon cinnamon
3 3/4 teaspoons baking powder
1 1/4 teaspoon salt
3 cups diced apples
1 cup chopped walnuts
1 Tablespoon butter or cooking spray

Yield: 2 dozen
Time: 20 minutes

Instructions:

Wash, peel and dice the apples into a large mixing bowl. Add the juice concentrate, applesauce, egg and oil. Do not mix the apple juice concentrate with water. Use it directly from the can, frozen or thawed. This is a good substitute for sugar.

Add remaining ingredients. Mix all ingredients together using a wooden spoon. Be sure the flour is well blended with the other ingredients. Grease a large rectangular baking dish with butter or cooking spray. Pour in the mixture and spread it around with a wooden spoon so that it covers the bottom of the pan. Bake at 350 degrees for 35 minutes or until the Apple Squares are golden brown. When they are done, remove them from the oven and cool them for about 15 minutes before you cut them.

Baked Peaches

This is an easy and delicious recipe that doesn't take much time. Serve with vanilla ice cream or yogurt.

You'll need:
- a can opener
- measuring cups and spoons
- a medium-size baking dish
- oven mitts

Ingredients:

4 canned peach halves. Use the kind packed in fruit juice instead of sugar
2 Tablespoons chopped walnuts
2 Tablespoons honey
1/8 teaspoon allspice

Yield: 2 servings
Time: 20 minutes

Instructions:

Preheat to 350 degrees. Place the peach halves cut side up in a shallow baking dish. In a small bowl combine walnuts, honey and allspice. Mix well and sprinkle over the peach halves. Bake for 20 minutes. Set aside to cool before serving.

IN PLACE OF ICE CREAM, SNACK ON WHOLESOME YOGURT, IT'S FULL OF VITAMINS AND CALCIUM.

Easy Raspberry Trifle

Pete fools everyone with this special recipe. It looks very fancy and hard to make but it's really very easy.

You'll need:
- a glass bowl with deep sides for assembling
- a mixing bowl for pudding
- electric mixer

measuring cups and spoons

Ingredients:

2 medium-sized apples
2 small containers lowfat vanilla yogurt
1/2 cup raspberry jam sweetened without sugar
1 pint fresh raspberries

Yield: 4 servings
Time: 15 minutes

Instructions:
Slice the apple and remove seeds.
Line the bottom of the serving bowl with apple slices. Using a dab of yogurt, stick apples to the side of the serving bowl all the way around.
Add 1/2 of the yogurt to the dish, spreading it evenly to cover the whole bottom. In a small bowl, stir the jam and raspberries together and spoon 1/2 of the mixture over the yogurt in the serving dish.
Cover that with more apple slices and add another layer of yogurt, using all that's left.
Top with the remaining jam mixture. Cover with plastic wrap.
Chill it in the refrigerator for 1 hour.

Upside Down Fruit Crunch

A topsy-turvy dessert that's fun to make and good to eat. This recipe is really good with raspberries or blueberries. Pineapple works too.

CRUNCH!

You'll need:
- an 8-inch square baking dish
- measuring cups
- small and medium-size mixing bowls
- a wooden spoon
- oven mitts

Ingredients:

3 cups fresh or frozen fruit
1/3 cup fruit juice concentrate
1/2 cup chopped pecans
2 eggs
1/2 cup butter
1 cup all-purpose flour

Yield: 8 servings
Time: Prep time is about 15 minutes

Instructions:
Grease an 8-inch square baking dish. Place the fruit in the bottom of the pan. It's okay to use canned pineapple but be sure to drain it first. Mix the nuts and 1/2 of the juice concentrate together in a small bowl and spread over the fruit. Set aside.

In a medium-size mixing bowl, combine the eggs, butter, flour and remaining juice concentrate and mix well with the wooden spoon.

Spread the mixture over the fruit. Bake at 325 degrees for 1 hour.

When the cake is done, remove it from the oven. Run a butter knife around the edges, then place a flat plate on top of the cake pan. Turn it over. Be careful, the cake pan will be very hot. Let the cake rest for 10 minutes before removing the pan. Cool for another 30 minutes before eating.

APPLE SLICES DIPPED IN PEANUT BUTTER MAKE A GREAT SWEET TREAT. TRY THIS WITH BANANAS TOO.

Piggy on a Stick

Rosa's favorite Popsicle is made with yogurt so she gets lots of good calcium. These little pigs are very tasty and this recipe makes enough to share with friends.

PIGGY ON A STICK

You'll need:
- 8 small paper cups
- 8 Popsicle sticks
- a small mixing bowl
- a wooden spoon
- measuring cups

Ingredients:

2 cups vanilla yogurt
1 12-ounce can apple-cranberry or cranberry-raspberry juice concentrate

Yield: 8 pops
Time 10 minutes

Instructions:
In a small bowl, mix together the yogurt and juice concentrate. Don't add water to the juice. Pour the mixture into the small cups. Cover the paper cups with aluminum foil and then insert the Popsicle sticks through the foil to keep it straight. Freeze until firm. When they are ready to eat, dip the cup in warm water just to the rim. Leave three seconds. This will loosen the cup so you can pop the piggy out easily.